Victorian Sheffield Entertainment

Researched by John Smith

Revised and edited by
Mike Gardner and Pat Braunton

Sheffield Theatre History Research Group

Published and printed by
Arc Publishing and Print
166 Knowle Lane
Sheffield S11 9SJ
Telephone 07809 172 872
email chris@arcbooks.co.uk
www.sheffieldbooks.co.uk

Dedication

This book is dedicated to the memory of John Smith who, sadly, died before it could be completed. He left behind a draft and a huge volume of meticulously detailed research.
This is his book.

Contents

Henry Irving

Dan Leno

Part 3   The Concert Halls

Jenny Lind

Part 4   And the Rest –
Something for Everyone

Annie Oakley

Appendix

References

Numbered notes refer to items in the press
and can be found on page 163.

All other references are marked by one or more stars
and can be found at the foot of the appropriate page.

Prologue

Our story of entertainment in Victorian Sheffield begins in 1843, the year the town became a municipal borough, and ends in 1893 when the borough became a city. It tells of a town growing at an astonishing rate and its attempts to entertain the vast numbers that were pouring in. It takes us to the mainstream theatres which often struggled to survive yet boasted some of the biggest stars of the day – among them the great William Macready, the Americans Edwin Forrest and Geneviève Ward, Italy's Adelaide Ristori and most famous of all, Henry Irving. We go to the Music Halls of West Bar where a very young Dan Leno trod the boards of the 'Britannia'. We visit the concert halls where audiences were thrilled by top opera stars like Jenny Lind and Adelina Patti, where huge numbers scrambled and fought to hear the American evangelists Sankey and Moody and where, all too often, Charles Hallé found himself playing to rows of empty seats.

We meet the remarkable Tommy Youdan, the local impresario whose enormous music halls and theatres were wonderfully successful. Some of the names we come across – Charles Dickens, Lillie Langtry, PT Barnum – will be familiar. Others like Mme Ohio, 'the Bearded Lady', and Miss Florence Wriggbitte, 'the great Female Tenor', are probably deservedly forgotten – yet they too are part of our story.

We spend some time in Sheffield's parks where Blondin, fresh from his conquest of the Niagara Falls, walked his tightrope. We go to the elaborate and brightly lit circuses which made regular visits to the town. We share the excitement when Buffalo Bill and Annie Oakley appeared in their Wild West Show. And we also find entertainment on offer in some unlikely places – vestry halls, temperance halls and the huge army drill halls.

Above all our story is about the people of Sheffield for surely their taste in entertainment helps to define them and gives us all some idea of what it was to be a Victorian in this fast growing town.

1

Charles Dillon – without doubt Sheffield's favourite
Victorian actor

Part 1
The Theatres

The Theatre Royal, the Adelphi,
the Surrey and the Alexandra

The Theatre Royal

The theatrical scene

Our story begins in 1843, just six years after the young Queen Victoria came to the throne, when the townships of Sheffield, Attercliffe, Brightside, Ecclesall and Hallam were brought together to form a single municipal borough. It was also the year when a new act of parliament brought fundamental alterations to the way Britain's theatres were organized and helped to provide a springboard for changes to Sheffield's theatrical scene. The most important change meant that performances no longer had to include music in order to obtain a licence from provincial magistrates. Also, if it chose to do so, any playhouse in Britain could call itself 'Theatre Royal'.[*]

Improved transport, particularly the rapid growth of the railways, began to transform the nature and content of entertainment but, for the most part, theatres carried on much as they had done since Sheffield's only playhouse first opened its doors in the 1760s. Drama in provincial theatres was still mainly provided by stock companies – groups of actors who would perform at a theatre throughout the season. The group would be familiar with a number of well-known plays and, when visiting stars came, the company would fill in all the minor parts and some major ones – often with little or no rehearsal. Top performers made very good money but in general actors and stage crews were not well paid and everyone relied on 'benefit' performances where the whole of an evening's takings were made available to supplement their incomes . Life upon the wicked stage was never easy.

Although the 1843 Theatres Act should have made life easier, Sheffield was not renowned as a culture-loving town and indeed managing a theatre there had always been something of a poisoned chalice. Lessees regularly fell behind with their rent. Proprietors, fearing for their dividends, held back on investment and it was often left to the poor lessee to fund any improvements to the décor, scenery and stage machinery. There was resistance from the non-conformist churches who saw theatricals as a threat to social morality and a Church of England clergyman, the vociferous Rev Thomas Best, preached regularly on the

---

[*] Details of the various Theatre Acts can be found in the Appendix.

subject.[*] Initially, magistrates responded to these pressures and granted a licence to just one theatre at a time for a maximum of twelve weeks.

A traditional playhouse

Sheffield's only licensed playhouse, stood at the corner of Tudor Street and Arundel Street on a site it shared with the Assembly Rooms. For a while it continued to call itself 'the Theatre' and did not seem to be in a rush to add 'Royal' to its title. It was still the same old Georgian playhouse which had opened in 1762[**].Not much had been spent on maintenance or improvements and backstage and front of house were both in a sorry state. Over the years there had not been much competition. Apart from the Music Hall, a concert hall round the corner in Surrey Street, and equestrian shows at the Royal Amphitheatre in the Cattle Market, the Theatre had grown used to having things pretty much its own way. Lack of competition breeds complacency and the old theatre had been content to muddle along for most of its eighty year history. Yet this ageing playhouse must be seen as central to our story of the development of entertainment in nineteenth-century Sheffield. Despite increased competition, problems caused by parsimonious proprietors and, at times, rank bad management, the old playhouse was still there at the end of the century and could make a reasonable claim to be Sheffield's premier theatre . Indeed it was still going strong until the 1930s when it was finally destroyed by fire.

On the face of it, Sheffield was ripe for an expansion of its theatrical activities. Its population was ten times greater than when the Theatre first opened and there was now a well-educated middle class. But Sheffield audiences seemed content with the old theatre which somehow still managed to create the illusion of a brightly-lit palace of entertainment and provide a welcome escape from the humdrum routine of daily life in a dirty industrial town.[***] Programmes largely consisted of contemporary comedies and melodramas, a few more serious plays and a lot of Shakespeare – very often performed in versions adapted to include music and song. An evening's

---

[*] A detailed account of Best's opposition can be found in Sheffield History Theatre Research Group, *Georgian Theatre in Sheffield,* Sheffield 2003.
His opposition to theatrical entertainment continued until his death in 1869.
[**] *Georgian Theatre in Sheffield* gives an account of earlier developments.
[***] The Theatre was one of the first theatres outside London to install gas lighting.

programme would usually consist of a tragedy, a comedy or farce, a burletta (a kind of musical farce) and a number of other short items.

Early managers – Robertson and Sloan

In 1843, when William Robertson became the first manager of the new era, he began cautiously but it was not long before he bowed to public pressure and invested in a number of famous actors including Charles Kean and his wife Ellen Tree, Samuel Butler and William Macready. Advertisements for Butler's *Macbeth* announced brand new scenery and 'the whole of Locke's music with an extra chorus engaged'.[*]

Georgian actors — William Macready and Charles and Ellen Kean

John Sloan took over in 1845, the year when the 'Theatre' finally decided to be known as 'The Theatre Royal'[**]. He too brought in big names – Helena Faucit, the comedy actress Mrs Fitzwilliam and the world famous ballerina,

---

[*] 'Locke's Music', written for Georgian productions of *Macbeth* continued to be popular for many years and indeed was still being used in Sheffield in the 1890s. In fact it was probably not written by Locke.

[**] Ironically, the Theatre's first real rival, the 'Royal Amphitheatre' in the Cattle Market was able to call itself 'Royal' from its opening day in 1838 because, as a venue for circus and equestrian entertainments, it did not need a dramatic licence from the magistrates.

Marie Taglione who danced *La Sylphide.* She gave just one performance and attracted a huge audience although prices were high: 'Boxes – six shillings, Pit – three shillings, Gallery – one shilling and sixpence with no half price'.

Ladies with legs: Mme Vestris famous for her 'breeches roles', and Marie Taglione who was the first dancer to wear a tutu

The autumn of 1845 also saw the first of many visits to Sheffield by the outstanding American actress Charlotte Cushman. Popular among her many Shakespearian roles was her Romeo with her sister Susan as Juliet. Tall and statuesque, Charlotte was very good at tackling male characters – and Sheffield audiences flocked to see her. 'Unqualified and decided success!' said the playbills, 'she having been hailed with the loudest applause ever heard within the walls of the Theatre'. She remained a Sheffield favourite for many years. Another talented lady was welcomed back for her final visit. Madame Vestris , a great beauty with a magnificent singing voice, excelled in burlesque and was famous for her 'breeches' roles. Sadly she was continually beset by financial problems and was often obliged to raise money by one-night-stands in the provinces.

Sloan's star-studded season ended in April 1846, with a performance by Edwin Forrest, one of the finest American tragic actors of the nineteenth century. He thrilled his audience in the title role of *King Lear,* a play which, because of George III's health problems, was seldom performed in this country during the last years of his reign, and had remained out of fashion.

American stars — Edwin Forrest and Charlotte Cushman, seen here with her sister Susan as Romeo and Juliet

Enter Charles Dillon – 'exactly what acting should be'

Charles Dillon became the new manager in October 1846. He burst upon Sheffield's theatrical scene as the hero of the popular French play, *Don César de Bazan* – and began a relationship with the town which was to last for the next thirty five years. Dillon was a handsome man, sporting an imperial beard and moustache, which was said to hide a slight deformity of the mouth. He was a capable manager and a very competent actor. Indeed Charles Dickens described his playing in *A Hard Struggle* as 'exactly what acting should be – nature itself'. An additional bonus was that Dillon brought his wife, Sarah Conquest, with him. Mrs Dillon, an accomplished actress, proved to be popular with Sheffield audiences and many of her performances drew enthusiastic reviews from the local press.

Sheffield had high expectations of Dillon, who had previously been a huge success as lessee of the Theatre Royal, Windsor. To some extent overcrowding and other first-night problems detracted from his performance – but the audience loved him. The *Independent* reported that

> a large number of pleasure-seekers was assembled at an early period, waiting for the unbarring of the doors, and anxious to secure good places. The pit and gallery were speedily filled, and the boxes were tenanted by a respectable company. It soon became apparent that the audience was too closely packed. The heat and noise became insupportable and cries of distress from the gallery interrupted the early part of the performance..It was exceedingly wrong to take money at the doors after the theatre was full.[1]

8

With a tragedian as lessee and leading actor the plays of Shakespeare were bound to feature largely in Dillon's opening season. As well as the usual favourites, they included the rarely performed *King John*. For the most part, things went well and his farewell speech was full of confidence. The receipts of the past season were proof of a growing taste for musical and dramatic entertainments in Sheffield though the largest sales were to the pit. As had happened many times before, the well-to-do whose seats in the boxes would have cost three or four times as much as those in the pit, all too often stayed away.

In the autumn of 1847, Dillon joined forces with Henry Widdicombe as joint manager. They promised 'a new company, new and splendid scenery, new and magnificent costumes, two new pieces and a numerous and efficient band'. There were some new plays and less Shakespeare though Sarah Anderton, a local girl, was given the chance to play Juliet.[*] Sheffield knew how to look after its own and there was a 'Grand Fashionable Night' in her honour. In the same year audiences at the Royal were treated to their first season of opera. Despite popular programmes and top singers this was a complete flop – but interest eventually grew and by the 1880s there was a well established demand for both grand opera and light operetta.

Overall, Dillon's management of the Royal had got off to a good start but things were beginning to happen down by the Cattle Market which were to have a profound effect on Sheffield's first theatre.

Competition from the Adelphi

Over on Blonk Street, not far from the Cattle Market, stood the Royal Amphitheatre. Built in 1838, it was a large, handsome building with a huge circus ring and, significantly, a decent sized proscenium stage. Because of its down-market location, it had never enjoyed much success and had posed no threat to the Royal until 1847, when the magistrates quite unexpectedly granted it a licence to perform drama. John Woodward, a vigorous new manager, built a new stage and added comfortable stalls giving him a clear advantage over the Royal where the audience still sat on pit benches. He renamed the building 'The Adelphi' and opened in time for the Christmas holiday season on 27 December 1847.

---

[*] Sarah Anderton was the niece of the editor of the Sheffield newspaper, *The Iris*.

William Farren

For the next thirteen years events down at Blonk Street had a profound effect on the fortunes of the Royal and for much of that time the two theatres were in direct competition. The Royal had the advantage of a central location, and its history and tradition encouraged a degree of support from the local press but the Adelphi had greater capacity and was able to keep prices low. In the end, however, it was the Royal which prevailed. A succession of managers failed to turn the Adelphi into a going concern and in 1859 it closed. During this time the Royal managed to consolidate its role. When John Faucit Saville took over in 1848, he spruced up the auditorium so that 'ladies now need not fear spoiled dresses in their visits to this place of amusement.' Crowd pleasers were engaged including William Farren, an excellent comic actor, and Mrs Moreton-Brookes who appeared in *Peeping Tom or, Lady Godiva's Ride Through Coventry* with Vienna her 'highly-trained steed'. Saville's theatre could also now lay claim to a truly 'royal' connection when Mrs Faucit Saville, C B Diddear, and other members of his company were invited by Queen Victoria to appear in a number of performances at Windsor Castle.

When Saville stood down, Charles Dillon returned followed by John Caple, another experienced manager – both failed. Then came a big surprise when, just before Easter 1853, Thomas Youdan, owner of a huge music hall in West Bar, stepped in to fill the gap. Youdan was almost certainly the most important, the most influential and the most successful figure in the development of Victorian theatre in Sheffield. He immediately got things moving and, ignoring seasonal niceties, staged the pantomime *Cinderella* before large and appreciative audiences. But the Royal was in a dilapidated condition with inadequate stage machinery and poor scenery– a small Georgian playhouse in the middle of a fast growing industrial town. Thomas Youdan, a hard-headed businessman, did not renew his lease.

Coleman and Johnson— new management and hope for the Royal

On 29 October 1853, an announcement appeared in the *Independent* which at last offered some positive encouragement:

THEATRE ROYAL, SHEFFIELD. The Patrons of the Drama are Respectfully informed that this Establishment, having been thoroughly cleansed and newly decorated in the First Style of Art will Open for the Season on Monday Next, October 31, under the Management of Messrs John Coleman and S Johnson. Knowles' Admired Comedy THE HUNCHBACK. PAS SEUL (GRANDE) by Mademoiselle Theodore. OCCASIONAL ADDRESS by Mr Coleman. THE NATIONAL ANTHEM by the Entire Company. To conclude with the popular Comedietta of THE BRITISH LEGION. Prices; Dress Boxes 2s 6d; Half Price at about 9 p.m. Is 6d; Pit Is. Gallery 6d.

The press welcomed these developments and also hoped to see better behaviour:

Perhaps this is the most fitting time to call attention to the disorderly conduct of some of those who frequent the gallery of this place. It is a notorious fact that from the gallery frequently issue sounds altogether unfit for decent ears. This nuisance is quite as objectionable to the majority of the gallery auditors as to those who visit the pit and boxes. For want of proper preventive means a few reckless youths are permitted to annoy and to disgust the respectable portions of the audience. So intolerable have these become that in some cases families keep aloof from the theatre and refuse to run the risk of having their ears polluted with filthy language...... If Messrs. Coleman and Johnson desire to perform before audiences of respectability, by timely precaution, they should suppress any attempted outrage.[2]

And the new managers appeared to have had some effect for the local press were soon able to report a significant improvement in the behaviour of the gallery. Egged on by the *Independent,* they announced that 'after new year's week children in arms would not be admitted'. However, a similar injunction at London's Sadler's Wells had led to some babies being brought in cunningly disguised as parcels – and Sheffield audiences may well have been tempted to follow suit.

Coleman loved spectacles and early in the season he staged a triumphant production of Byron's colourful drama *Sardanapalus*. As well as the ever popular dramas, opera was now all the rage with houses packed to overflowing. The proprietors were highly impressed and at last gave the go-ahead for the long awaited major refurbishment of the old theatre. They promised to renew Coleman's lease when the alterations were complete but although Coleman and Johnson made a good team, they had faced financial difficulties. New scenery, new costumes and improvements to the antiquated stage machinery had proved very costly and in their second year the joint managers were summonsed for unpaid wages.

The Theatre Royal rebuilt

In fact, work did not begin until 26 March 1855 and the task was not an easy one. The aim was to increase capacity but there was little that could be done to enlarge the exterior of the building. Arundel Street ran along one side, there was private property on the other and at the rear were the Assembly Rooms. The architects, Flockton and Son of Sheffield, decided that the only solution was to gut the theatre completely. They did manage to enlarge the foyer a little by building out over the pavement – and this completely changed the appearance of the old theatre. Gone was the elegant eighteenth-century façade and now, right across the front of the building, there was a cast iron and glass canopy to protect the hats and hairstyles of the carriage folk from inclement weather. Inside, the old Georgian Theatre was completely transformed. The pit was excavated and enlarged and some of the boxes were removed and replaced by a dress circle for the better class patrons. There was an upper circle and a new gallery which was described as 'one of the best in the kingdom for comfort'. The whole interior was decorated in the style of Louis XIV with new upholstery and new gas fittings installed by the resident engineer from Covent Garden. There was a new stage with better dressing rooms as well as a green room. The building had partial central heating using hot water pipes topped up with fires and stoves. Water closets were installed for the first time – to everyone's relief. Inside and out Sheffield's Theatre Royal was now a typical Victorian playhouse.

The structural changes meant a huge increase in capacity. The new pit had bench accommodation for about nine hundred with the first three rows nearest the stage partitioned off to form a hundred orchestra stalls with upholstered seats. The dress circle and boxes seated about four hundred and there were about twelve hundred cheaper seats in the upper circle and gallery. The Royal now held around two thousand five hundred – although it still could not match the three thousand at the Adelphi. The final bill came to £3,500 (the original estimate was £2,700) so the proprietors did not receive dividends for several years. Now a rent of £400 a year was proposed by the proprietors and Coleman and Johnson were unable to afford it. And so it was Charles Dillon who became the first manager of the 'new' Theatre. Sheffield theatergoers could scarcely wait to see the inside of their prestigious new playhouse so Dillon had an easy time. In funds for once he decided to take over the Adelphi as well – but this venture was short-lived. By October 1856, facing stiff competition from Coleman, who had taken over the running of the Adelphi, Dillon also gave up the management of the Royal. Yet he seems to have found it difficult to stay away from Sheffield. A year later he was back – this time as an actor. For the next two years managers at the Royal, including the actor-dramatist Charles Webb, struggled to keep the place open. There were a few highlights. In 1857 the famous Adelaide Ristori played Medea and opera drew decent audiences. But it was Dillon's visits, in favourites such as *Othello* and *Louis XI,* which kept the ship afloat. Nevertheless the theatre was open for only eleven of its advertised twenty two weeks. Then Dillon was declared bankrupt and

decided to try his luck in Australia. Of course, there had to be a farewell performance – and what a performance it was. A huge audience turned up to see him appear in *Ingomar* and *The Lady of Lyons* and the evening became chaotic.[3] The noise from the overcrowded gallery forced the actors to shout so loudly that people sitting near the front were deafened and some even climbed into the boxes to escape the din. This final marathon lasted five hours.

Adelaide Ristori as Medea with her children

Stability at the Royal: Charles and Ellen Pitt

Webb managed to keep going until February 1859. He was succeeded by Alfred Davis, a highly regarded comic actor and playwright who brought in well known actors including Charlotte Vandenhoff and her husband Thomas Swinbourne – and a star of the future, Marie Wilton. The talented dancer, Mrs Ramsden, wife of the company scene painter, also appeared in several shows and was fast becoming a great favourite in Sheffield's theatres. [*] The hit of the season, *A Tale of Two Cities,* came to Sheffield just a couple of months after its London debut. Things were looking up.

Charlotte Vandenhoff as Juliet

The Royal's fortunes had improved while Davis was in charge – but unfortunately he left after just one season. However, the proprietors now found the ideal man to provide a much needed period of stability. Charles Dibden Pitt, together with his wife Ellen, succeeded in running the theatre for nine years– a record exceeded only by William M'Cready in the Regency period. Both Pitts came from a theatrical background. Charles was an experienced manager and Ellen a capable administrator.

The new manager began well. As the century progressed, Sheffield became more prosperous and increasingly dirty and almost certainly began to resemble Dickens' 'Coke Town' 'where nature was as strongly bricked out as killing airs and gasses were bricked in'. [**] The first task for nearly every lessee at the Royal was to spend as much as he could afford on a thorough clean. So Pitt drew on his limited resources to give the auditorium a lick of paint – and grubby white and gold gave way to brighter colours. A new act drop, showing Queen Elizabeth watching a play by Shakespeare, added dignity and William Ramsden prepared brand new scenery. The

---

[*] Mrs Ramsden, her famous skipping-rope dance and her equally talented daughters were always in demand in theatres and music halls all over town.
[**] Charles Dickens, *Hard Times,* reprinted Penguin Books, London 1994, p56.

season opened on 20 October 1860 with several heavyweight dramas including *Macbeth, Othello, King Lear* (with Mrs Pitt as the Fool), *The Man in the Iron Mask* and *Catherine Howard.*

Pitt assembled a distinguished company and soon began to attract good houses. Then, in February 1861, he came up with something special. Dion Boucicault's *The Colleen Bawn* was the play that every theatregoer in the country wanted to see. Full of exciting incidents, it culminated in a great sensation scene where the heroine, drowning in Lake Killarney was saved at the very last moment by the comic man. Press and public alike were bowled over by the elaborate scenic effects and the play ran at the Royal for an amazing fifty one consecutive performances.

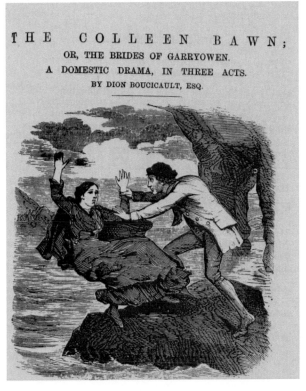

THE COLLEEN BAWN;

OR, THE BRIDES OF GARRYOWEN.

A DOMESTIC DRAMA, IN THREE ACTS.

BY DION BOUCICAULT, ESQ.

In his curtain speech on the final night of the season, Pitt enthusiastically spelt out his achievements. He had brought before the audience the best company of any provincial theatre in the country. He had paid higher salaries than any previous manager – and he owed nothing. He was equally keen to congratulate the people of Sheffield. He had appealed to his gallery friends to conduct themselves as British workmen knew how to do, and they had thoroughly responded to his appeal in a dignified manner.[4]

Pitt felt secure enough to take on a three year lease at £450 per annum and opened a month earlier than usual in September 1861. He continued to show good judgement in his choice of plays including another Boucicault

15

blockbuster, *The Octoroon,* set in America's deep south which attracted huge audiences. Pitt was also prepared to fight to maintain his monopoly. He saw off an attempt by the Music Hall in Surrey Street to turn itself into an opera house. He informed on Thomas Youdan when he put on plays without

a licence at his West Bar Music Hall — and when Youdan tried to obtain a stage licence it was Pitt who made sure that he did not get one. He also invested in major structural alterations. The ceiling was raised and new ventilators installed in a further attempt to cure the stifling heat problems. The gallery was altered to squeeze in an extra two hundred seats and the pit benches were replaced by individually numbered seats[*]. A wire screen across the front of the gallery prevented the front row from displaying the soles of their boots to the boxes.

Dion Boucicault

Later that season Pitt broke with tradition by moving the opening night of the pantomime from Boxing Day to Christmas Eve. Usually, opening nights on Boxing Day were far from pleasant. A huge, inebriated, smelly gallery audience often made so much noise that it was impossible to hear the short curtain-raiser which preceded the main event. On Christmas Eve 1861 things were very different:

> Nothing could be more orderly than were "the Gods" — no fights, no heat, no tobacco smoke, no oranges! There was but a limited call for ginger-beer and no gin.

Pitt's strategy worked — and the pantomime was a huge success. The following year he even tried to do something about the smell. The advertisement for the pantomime promised something special:

---

[*] Seats were not numbered in London theatres until 1884. A playbill for Sheffield's Adelphi theatre on 2 October 1857 advertised 'seats reserved and numbered with no additional charge for booking'. See *Georgian Theatre in Sheffield* p79.

16

LITTLE RED RIDING HOOD
HARLEQUIN BOY BLUE, THE WOLF FIEND
AND THE
BUTTERFLY FAIRIES OF THE GOLDEN
FUCHSIA GROVE
As written and produced under the Direction of Mr. WYBERT
REEVE. The music arranged by Mr. J. W. ALLWOOD. The
magnificent Scenery, mixed with rural delights, by Mr. J,B,
Lennox will eclipse all former efforts in beauty and splendour.

In the Beautiful Fairy Scene of
THE FUCHSIA GROVE AND BUTTERFLY'S HAUNT
"An invisible perfume will hit the sense
from the adjacent wharfs" - *Shakespeare.*
BEING A NOVEL AND EXPENSIVE INVENTION, SUP –
LIED DIRECT FROM M. EUGENE RIMMEL,
96, Strand, London; Its first introduction into Sheffield, filling
The House with Delicious Sweetness

The house filled with delicious sweetness provided by the very expensive
M. Rimmel! What more could one ask?

Wybert Reeve

Overall Pitt's first few years in charge had gone well and much of his
success was due to the support he received from his wife, his daughters Fanny and Kate and, in particular, Wybert Reeve. Reeve stayed at the Royal for four years and in that time displayed his amazing talent for all things theatrical. He acted, he wrote and supervised the pantomimes. He stage-managed. When a play was required to show off a special ghost effect – he wrote one. Reeve won over the press. The *Independent* praised his ability as an author and described him as 'the best stage manager our theatre ever had; a most accomplished comedian; and a gentleman whose friendship is very much esteemed'[5]. The audiences loved him and it was a sad day for the Royal when Reeve finally moved on.

Pantomimes

There is little doubt that the annual pantomime was an important part of Sheffield's theatrical scene for a successful show provided much needed cash and enabled many a struggling manager to survive. The pantomime traditionally opened on Boxing Day and, if all went well, the manager would hope that it would still be running well into March and enable him to put on decent shows for the rest of that season and the beginning of the next. In 1861 the Royal claimed that, by 7 January, '22,900 persons have already witnessed our gorgeous pantomime'.

Eighteenth century pantomimes generally presented stock characters and situations derived from commedia dell'arte with Harlequin and Columbine in the leading roles. As the nineteenth century wore on this element became increasingly less important. Yet as late as the 1890s some pantomimes continued to include a 'harlequinade'. Many of the stories would be familiar to today's theatre-goers - *Cinderella, Aladdin, Sinbad the Sailor, Babes in the Wood, The Fair One with the Golden Locks.*, There were also some more unusual titles – *Valentine and Orson, Nicodemus and the Good Fairy Green, Beauty and Grace* and *Bluebeard* – complete with a ballet of headless wives!

The world of the pantomime is infinitely flexible so it was always possible to add a little local colour. No doubt those who watched *Cinderella* at the Royal in 1882 were delighted to find that the 'Palace of the Peak' was an 'excellent picture of Chatsworth House by night'.

In the latter half of Victoria's reign there were two main developments. Better technology meant that more elaborate scenic effects were now possible – and pantomime audiences loved spectacular settings and magical transformation scenes. Then, in the 1880s, Augustus Harris began to include top music hall stars in his Drury Lane pantomimes and provincial theatres soon followed suit. These performers were often very expensive. When Jenny Hill was the the principal boy in *Robinson Crusoe* at the Royal in 1886 she was paid fifty pounds a week.

Pantomimes were not confined to the main theatres. Large travelling circuses would usually stage a pantomime if they were in Sheffield over the Christmas period. In theory, since they did not have a theatre licence, they were not allowed to include dialogue in their performances. But it seems highly likely that many of them did and consequently provided strong competition for the mainstream theatres. The temporary structures in which they performed were often highly elaborate affairs and their pantomimes were full of wonderful spectacular effects. A company which included acrobats, high-wire specialists, trapeze artists, performing animals and clowns had all the ingredients for a successful pantomime. Many a theatre manager must have been worried when a circus rolled into town.

'Lord Dundreary'

Pitt's third season ran for 234 nights and he presented no fewer than 216 different plays. The programme included a great many sensation dramas and *Bavin's Brow* a new play by a local author, J S Fox — with Fox himself in the cast. The top billing, however, was reserved for Edward Sothern as Lord Dundreary in Tom Taylor's *Our American Cousin*. Sothern's performance, complete with 'Dundreary Whiskers,' could have been sold out several times over.

Edward Compton also brought revivals of tried-and-tested English comedies such as *She Stoops to Conquer, The Rivals* and *The School for Scandal*. The 1863 autumn season opened with Tom Taylor's *The Ticket-of-Leave Man*. The play, believed to be the first to feature a detective, is a serious attempt to explore the problems facing a young man recently released from prison. The local press were unimpressed but the public ignored the poor reviews and gave it a rapturous reception.

Edward Compton

Pitt's troubles probably began with a royal wedding. On 10 March 1863, Edward, Prince of Wales was to marry Princess Alexandra and the Royal, the Music Hall in Surrey Street, the Mechanics' Institute and Youdan's Surrey Music Hall in West Bar all decided to mark the event by holding masked balls. The Royal's pit benches were removed and a prefabricated dance floor was installed at stage level. Festoons of flowers decorated the boxes and dress circle, lit by a new chandelier. It all seemed rather splendid:

The appearance of the ball, when the room was full and dancing going on was very picturesque. Some ladies were in costume and others wore masks. Among the gentlemen were Brigands, Turks, Spaniards, Sailors, Swedes, Louis Quatorze, Tyrolese, Mexicans and Monks, with amateur Hamlets, Mercurys, Sweeps and Monkeys, and it is scarcely too much to say that all enacted their parts well, and all appeared to dance as if it were a duty.'[6]

Unfortunately 'two gentlemen members of a religious body' reported horrific stories of lewd and disorderly women (some of them smoking in public!) and idle and dissolute young men 'in their evil courses' and Pitt was summonsed. Charges were dismissed but Pitt's reputation had been damaged – and he had to pay the costs of the hearing.

Then, later that year, Thomas Youdan finally managed to get a drama licence for his lavishly equipped Surrey Music Hall in West Bar. Youdan immediately closed the hall and two days later, on 28 September, reopened it as the Surrey Theatre. Pitt was shocked. He reduced his prices to bring them into line with those at the Surrey – but while that vast theatre had a huge capacity and could afford low prices, the Royal most certainly could not. The American drama, *The Poor of New York,* did badly even though it had a strong cast, an exciting conflagration scene, and ridiculously low prices.

Worse was to follow. Towards the end of 1863, Sangers' Circus staged an equestrian Christmas pantomime. Pitt panicked and immediately tried to close it arguing that the Sangers were performing a play without a licence. The Magistrates disagreed – there was no dialogue so the show could not be called a 'play'. Pitt, unconvinced, still hoped to catch out the Sangers by sending spies to each performance. But the people of Sheffield loved their circuses and were distinctly peeved by Pitt's shenanigans. Feelings ran high – protesters took to the streets and Ellen Pitt was injured when a brick was thrown through their drawing room window. Pitt became more and more alarmed by the popularity of circuses and music halls and responded by introducing 'cheap nights' where all seats were half price. Like many others he had fallen into the discount trap and his finances, which had previously been so sound, began to worry him.

Although there was fierce competition between the Surrey and the Royal, early in 1864 they suddenly found themselves united in a common cause. On the night of Friday, 11 March two hundred and thirty seven lives were lost when the wall of the Dale Dyke dam burst and floodwater swept down through the town causing terrible damage and destruction. Miraculously, the music halls and theatres escaped unscathed and both the Royal and the Surrey set about helping out. Pitt's contribution was to put on two special performances to raise money and he also made the Royal available for a fund-raising effort by the Hallamshire Rifle Volunteers – a historical drama and a burlesque of *Macbeth.*

After the flood

This show was a huge success but later in the year Pitt made another big mistake. He decided to celebrate Shakespeare's tercentenary by holding another fancy dress ball. He should have known better. Once again licentious behaviour was reported and he found himself in court. The magistrates threatened to suspend his licence and the *Independent* regretted that 'on such an occasion the boards of our Theatre Royal should have been put to such a use'.[7]

Pitt's confidence was now at a low ebb. Boucicault's *The Streets of London* had been a huge hit in London and the news that Youdan was planning to stage an elaborate production, complete with a spectacular conflagration scene, was a real concern[*]. Pitt decided that he would literally fight fire with fire and he put on *The Mother's Dying Child* which also had a 'Great Conflagration' as well as 'Shocking Events, a Great Water Scene and the Most Terrific Final Scene ever attempted on any stage'. His production did well but in the event he need not have worried for a few days after *The Streets of London* opened, Youdan's theatre was completely destroyed by fire. There were no casualties but the actors and stagehands lost everything. Even Pitt felt moved to help them and raised £71 at a special benefit performance. Youdan, some £30,000 out of pocket, appeared to be finished but any sympathy felt by Pitt must have been tempered by a good deal of relief.[**]

---

[*] Earlier Pitt had staged *The Poor of New York,* the original version of the play, with little success.

[**] For an account of Youdan's theatres see pages 43-69.

Mrs Pitt takes over

Relief was short-lived, however. Youdan bounced back and reopened the disused Adelphi as the Alexandra Music Hall. Pitt's health deteriorated and he died on 21 February 1866. Mrs Pitt who had been keeping things going during her husband's illness now took over the lease – and struggled on for the next three years. She was ably supported by her four children and her charismatic wardrobe master, Oliver Cromwell, a man of enormous vitality who acted, stage managed and helped with administration. On top of all this he found time to play football for a local club and did much to promote the sport in Sheffield. He presented the Cromwell Cup to The Wednesday Football Club.[*]

Ellen Pitt did her best. She brought in the popular Montague Smythson as her leading man and engaged the French tragedienne, Mademoiselle Beatrice, for the first of many successful visits to Sheffield.   For a time Mrs Pitt managed to keep going but overall returns were poor. Tom Robertson's

'cup-and-saucer' comedy, *Society,* a huge hit in London, received a lukewarm response and Charles Kean and Ellen Tree's farewell visit was extremely disappointing. To make matters worse there was direct competition from Youdan who had not only obtained a theatre licence for the Alexandra but persuaded Oliver Cromwell to join him. Mrs Pitt had had enough. She gave her final performance as manager on 14 May 1869.[**]

Mlle Beatrice - a Sheffield favourite

---

[*] The world's first football trophy, The Youdan Cup was presented to Hallam in 1867. The Cromwell Cup was first presented in 1868.
[**] Mrs Pitt returned to Sheffield to perform at the Alexandra in 1871 and the Royal in 1883 and 1884.

Gomersal and Eldred

Despite ups and downs and the occasional near disaster, the Pitts' nine year struggle had left the old theatre in reasonable shape. The next five years saw two managers build new levels of prosperity. First came William Gomersal who took over in 1869 with his wife and family in tow – and from the start seemed to do everything right. He was well known in Sheffield having performed at both the Royal and the Adelphi. He gave the theatre a good clean and installed a new act drop depicting Amalfi. He shrewdly offered the premises, free of charge, to the Rev R Stainton for Sunday meetings, hymn singing and lectures, a move which was not only good for public relations but also show-cased the building to people who were not regular theatre-goers.

Gomersal introduced a wide range of drama opening with Mrs Henry Wood's *East Lynne,* the ultimate Victorian 'weepie.' There were visits by J L Toole and Dillon. There were musical attractions – The English Opera Company included Sheffield on its provincial tours and smaller companies provided lighter entertainment in the form of operettas and opera bouffe. And then there was *Fly,* a 'horse opera' from London's Surrey Theatre,

which starred the 'wonderful horse Etna – helped by Miss Edith Sandford'. In the final scene Miss Sandford and her trusty steed, hedged in by flames on all sides, rode to the rescue of the child of an Arab chief.

William Gomersal

When Charles Dickens died in 1870, Gomersal was quick to cash in and signed up Andrew Halliday's *Little Em'ly,* based on *David Copperfield*, hot from a successful run in London. There was more Dickens a few weeks later when Amy Sedgwick played Sergeant Buzfuz in the trial scene from *Pickwick Papers* – one 'of the finest delineations of character ever attempted by a lady'.[8] Public and press were delighted.

Henry Irving   *Barry Sullivan*
Irving would soon take over from Sullivan as the Victorians' most popular actor

In the summer of 1871, Henry Irving came to the Royal for the first time. Irving – the man of the moment – was fast establishing himself as one of the country's finest actors and everyone wanted to see him. He arrived in the middle of a heat wave to play Digby Grant in James Albery's *Two Roses.* In spite of the weather the Royal was packed.[9] Another celebrity, W S Gilbert, was persuaded to venture north in 1872 to see his mythological comedy, *Pygmalion and Galatea.* His appearance at the final curtain was greeted with 'rapturous applause'.[10]

Irving's lucrative visit financed the re-laying of the stage and the repainting of the auditorium. The Rev Stainton, who was still holding his Sunday services there, wrote to the *Independent* emphasizing that the newly decorated dress circle was now for ladies only and that gentlemen would be restricted to the pit and the gallery! By 1872, Gomersal had been so successful that the Royal's proprietors were anxious to get their hands on a share of his profits. When he applied to renew his lease, they demanded an extra hundred pounds which he grudgingly paid. Then they demanded another £250 for further redecoration. That was the last straw for Gomersal – and the Royal lost an outstanding manager. There is little doubt that the public realized what they were losing. Gomersal's farewell benefit was completely sold out and, because so many were turned away, the performance was repeated the following evening. In his speech from the stage he made it abundantly clear why he had been forced to leave. A further indication of his popularity came when, at the end of the evening, grateful employees presented him with a silver cup.

His successor, Joseph Eldred, began well. Taking over during another extremely hot summer, he immediately improved the ventilation and sightlines by replacing the chandelier, fitting a huge vent in the middle of the ceiling and lowering the footlights. He redecorated in a style 'chaste in the extreme' and provided a retiring room for ladies in the dress circle. There were excellent houses when the theatre reopened.

By the 1870s, thanks to the vast improvements in the railways network, touring productions were increasingly taking over from the resident stock companies. Eldred did bring in a couple of stars of the old school both of whom still required the support of stock companies. One, perhaps inevitably, was Charles Dillon. The other was the tragedian Barry Sullivan, generally still regarded as the outstanding actor of the day. Predictably, Sullivan's visit was a huge success yet Eldred remained convinced that the way forward lay with the touring companies.

Wilkie Collins

One such touring show was *The Woman in White,* an adaptation by Wilkie Collins of his celebrated novel, performed by the author's own company.[11] And Edwin Romaine brought to Sheffield the perfect play for a steel town in love with melodramas – *True as Steel,* the 'Great Northern Drama with its Great Sensation Scene of the Steam Hammer.' In a nicely judged ironic review the *Independent* commented that 'such a sweet plot was surely never devised by any playwright'. It also had something to say about the set:

The scenery, too, is highly appropriate. There is a representation of a large Sheffield ironworks. A river flows by the building – presumably the Don. But the water is depicted as of a pure deep blue; the banks of the stream are covered with golden sands and violet tinted mosses; while the sky is of a pure ethereal blue dotted with fleecy white clouds. All this is very natural, and nice and pleasant – only it won't go down with Sheffield people.[12]

But it did go down well. *True as Steel* played to packed houses and returned to the Theatre Royal many times.

Despite successes like these, it soon became apparent that Eldred's initial enthusiasm was quickly evaporating. There were a few highlights in 1873 including a popular return visit by Barry Sullivan. In September, the Carl Rosa Opera Company gave its first performance in Manchester and just a few weeks later it made the first of many visits to Sheffield. But otherwise the productions were generally dull and predictable. Eldred left in May 1874.

Sefton Parry moved in, made no impact at all, left after a few weeks and was replaced by L J Sefton. His stay was somewhat longer but equally unremarkable except for a speech, made on his first benefit night, in which he set out some of the problems facing a theatre manager in Sheffield. The speech was fully reported in the press:

> There is just now in Sheffield a great stir about the educational movement, but I do not think the value of the theatre as an educational institution is appreciated in the town. Lectures on Shakespeare are given by learned professors, and prominent citizens lend their aid to the movement, but when they are asked to lend the weight of their influence to the legitimate shrine of the drama, they shake their heads and say they never went to the theatre, they disapproved of it. It is a pity that gentlemen could not throw off their prejudices, until they did so Sheffield could not hold the same position as an artistic centre as other towns. [13]

THIS EVENING

THEATRE ROYAL SHEFFIELD

Sole and Responsible Manager... MR RICHARD YOUNGE

ENTERTAINMENT FOR SIX NIGHTS ONLY OF
MR and MRS. FRAYNE
AND THE
GREAT KENTUCKY RIFLE TEAM
Master FRANKIE FRAYNE
Assisted by JAMES M .BUTLER and ROBERT M. FRAYNE
And Introducing the Wonderful Frontier American
Dog, Jade
ON THIS MONDAY August 21 and DURING THE WEEK,
S I S L O C U M
Supported by MISS VIOLET ERRINGTON'S COMPANY

During the play Mr. Frayne will shoot an apple from his wife's head by the celebrated backward shot, placing his gun over his shoulder and taking a sight from the reflection of a six inch mirror , his back towards the mark.   Mrs. Clara Frayne will shoot an apple from her Husband's head making strictly an off-hand shot, a feat attempted by no other lady in the world.   Master Frankie, five years of age, will shoot a bird placed at random by his Father off-hand, a feat attempted by no other child.

Sefton would no doubt have been warmly applauded by dozens of his predecessors who throughout the Royal's entire history had battled against the odds to make ends meet. A year later, when things seemed to be improving, he died quite suddenly. He was buried in Ecclesall Churchyard. The Royal closed for a week. [14]

Richard Younge took over in July 1876, signed a three year lease at the exorbitant rate of £800 a year and immediately set about providing a wide variety of entertainment. In August 1876, The Great Kentucky Rifle Team presented *Si Slocum,* a piece designed to show off the sharp-shooting talents of the Frayne family – including five year old Master Frankie. Then, a month later, in complete contrast, came the Soldene Opera Bouffe Company whose repertoire included various light operas, Miss Emily Soldene singing 'the favourite melody " Silver threads among the gold"' and, for the first time in Sheffield, a performance each night of Gilbert and Sullivan's *Trial by Jury.* Then in November, there was chance to hear a world famous soprano, Thérèse Tietiens, give three performances with Her Majesty's Opera Company.[*]

Emily Soldene

John Coleman's acclaimed revival of *Henry V* began its provincial tour at the Royal in April 1877, generating much needed cash for further refurbishments and redecoration.^{**} The dress circle and pit refreshment bars were enlarged, the stage was re-laid and new machinery was fitted. The auditorium was redecorated in French grey, pink, white and gold. The following year the smart, newly decorated auditorium played host to three big events. August saw D'Oyly Carte bring a Gilbert and Sullivan opera to Sheffield for the first of many visits.

Now, as well as a reprise of *Trial by Jury,* there was full scale production of *The Sorcerer.*^{***} In September, the Carl Rosa Company were back with *Maritana, The Merry Wives of Windsor* and *The Bohemian Girl* and in November, there was a four day visit by Henry Irving. Since his previous visit he had enjoyed unprecedented success as Matthias in Leopold Lewis's *The Bells* and was now, without doubt, the country's most popular actor. His London Lyceum Company offered *Hamlet, Richard III* and, of course, *The Bells.* The Royal was packed.

Richard D'Oyly Carte

---

[*] Tietiens also performed at the Music Hall in Surrey Street– see page 96
^{**} Coleman had been made bankrupt again in 1876 but it had not taken him long to be back in business.
^{***} Audiences at the Royal loved Gilbert and Sullivan . Particular favourites included *The Yeomen of the Guard, Iolanthe, Patience* and *The Mikado.*

27

'An entirely new Theatre Royal'

In 1880, the Royal closed in June for yet another massive rebuilding programme. Although the last major work, carried out in 1855, had made improvements it had failed to correct many of the theatre's fundamental flaws. The proprietors called in the London theatre architect Charles J Phipps who prepared plans to increase the capacity by several hundred by removing the boxes completely and enlarging the dress circle. In addition, the gallery was to be improved by raising the roof by fifteen feet. All this did not come cheap. The cost of alterations, reseating, redecoration, and refitting gas pipes, had been estimated at £5,500 but rose to £8,000 on completion. However, it was well worth it. 'It is scarcely too much to say that an entirely new Theatre Royal has been erected upon a most attractive design, and the dingy home of the drama once possessed by the town has been converted into a well arranged place of amusement, elegantly appointed.'[15] Indeed the changes were so great that the theatre felt able to advertise itself as 'The New Theatre Royal' and it reopened with a bang on 1 November 1880 with a new manager, E Romaine Callender, in charge. It was a very grand affair – the national anthem was sung by a choir of a hundred voices conducted by Samuel Hadfield, and then the new lessee set out his good intentions in an inaugural speech: 'A theatre is not a church but I hope to make it an influence for good, a place where those who are wearied by the work of the day may find harmless recreation.'[16]

Callender's opening programme certainly offered plenty of variety. It began with *Le Voyage en Suisse,* a 'Parisian absurdity,' followed by *Henry V.* Then there was a 'wild west' play, *The Danites; or, the Heart of the Sierras*, a drama about a young girl's attempts to escape the clutches of a violent Mormon sect. This was followed by *DT or Lost by Drink* – a temperance melodrama written by the new manager himself. French burlesque, Shakespeare, the wild west and a temperance melodrama – there was surely something to please everyone.

Charles Dillon's final bow

After the usual pantomime, Charles Dillon returned, this time in a lavish production of *Macbeth*. Mrs Romaine Callender was his

28

Sporting   Celebrities

During the latter half of the nineteenth century,
Sheffield was very much involved in the development
of sport. Bramall Lane, which was used for both
cricket and football, opened in the fifties and played
host to a number of visiting county cricket teams –
and, indeed, in 1902 the ground staged the town's one
and only test match. For the most part the two major
theatres were pleased to welcome visiting teams.
When Richard Younge took over the Royal in 1876
one of his first tasks was to entertain some sporting
celebrities for W G Grace and his Gloucestershire
team turned up for a performance of a sensation
drama, *Dead to the World*. Then, two years later, the

visiting Australian tourists were in the audience for another good old-fashioned
melodrama, *Notice to Quit*. In 1882, the Australians were back in Sheffield and this
time several members of the team watched a programme of opera which included

Traditional Dress.

Bizet's *Carmen*. And the 1886 touring side
actually sponsored a production of a play
called *The Fancy Ball*.

The Australians were not the only sportsmen
to come to the Royal. Early in 1876 the
management were delighted when the
Canadian Gentlemen Amateur Lacrosse team,
accompanied by the Iroquois Indians, accepted
an invitation to watch a production of
Formosa — and the Indians promised to attend
in their native costume!

Not all theatre visits were a success. The night
after Grace and his Gloucestershire team
watched *Dead to the World* at the Royal, they
went along to the Alexandra to see *The Serf,
or Love Levels All,* by Tom Taylor — and
made a thorough nuisance of themselves. The *Independent* reported that
they were eventually induced to leave by the return of their ticket money —
they were, in fact, thrown out. There had been no reports of bad behaviour
when the team visited the Royal the night before – perhaps this time the
good Doctor and his chums had dined rather too well.

Lady Macbeth and there was a choir of a hundred witches singing Locke's music. However, this spectacular show proved to be Dillon's last. On 22 June 1881, he died at Hawick, aged sixty two, and Sheffield lost its most popular Victorian actor. For more than three decades, year in year out, Dillon had played all the major tragic roles and enthusiastic audiences had always come back for more.

Callender continued to provide a varied programme. First came *Imprudence* a new play by Arthur Wing Pinero. This was followed by appearances by some top class performers – Madame Ristori, the American tragedian Edwin Booth and another American, Geneviève Ward, who had starred in *Forget-me-Not* the stage hit of 1882. The local critic was impressed:

> Miss Genevieve Ward appears in her original character of "Stephanie" and gives a powerful interpretation of a part most difficult and exacting.[17]

But Geneviève found her visit to Sheffield most disappointing for it coincided with a smallpox epidemic and she played to very poor houses. In her memoirs she said that during her week in Sheffield she never saw the sun or blue sky.[*]

Top American performers – Edwin Booth and Geneviève Ward

---

[*] Geneviève Ward and Richard Whiteing: *Both Sides of the Curtain* , London 1918, p 168.

Callender's exciting time in charge came to an abrupt end in 1884 when, like so many of his predecessors, he was declared bankrupt. Amazingly no fewer than twenty seven applicants for the vacancy responded to the advertisement in the *Era.*[*] The delighted proprietors immediately raised the rent to a thousand a year and appointed W Henry Daw, manager of the Theatre Royal Cardiff. Daw's time at the Royal went reasonably well although unfortunately he made little profit overall. However, there were a few big successes.

One of these was when Lillie Langtry made a welcome return to Sheffield. She had earlier appeared at the Alexandra and audiences at the Royal were delighted to have a second chance to see the Prince of Wales' lady friend. Despite astronomical ticket prices she drew huge audiences.

In October,1885, the multi-talented American actress Minnie Palmer came to the Royal to play Tina in *My Sweetheart*. The play boasted 'a remarkable actress, a remarkable company and, a remarkable trio of managers'. Minnie certainly lived up to expectations. She showed she could act, dance and sing – and she was extremely pretty. 'It is doubtful whether any lady ever possessed such qualifications for success on stage in a part like that of Tina' wrote the *Independent* noting that throughout her performance there were 'frequent and, at the same time, spontaneous outbursts of applause.'[18] Sheffield audiences loved her and they also loved the play. 1888 saw Minnie playing Tina once again at the Royal and, during the very same week, Marie Montrose, a younger, very talented actress, receiving plaudits for her performance in *My Sweetheart* at the Alexandra.

Minnie Palmer — 'one of the brightest and liveliest beings that ever trod the thespian boards'.

---

[*] *The Era* was a weekly newspaper about theatre, actors, music hall, and all related matters. It was published and printed in London from 1837 to 1939.

Augustus Harris

Then 'Druriolanus', Augustus Harris, the manager of the Drury Lane Theatre, chose the Royal to launch his provincial tour of *A Run of Luck*, a racing melodrama. Excitement ran high and crowds gathered in Tudor Street to see the live 'properties' – racehorses, dogs and their keepers, taking exercise in the town centre during rehearsals. Every seat was soon sold and the delighted critic in the *Independent* was amazed to have witnessed a drama in which no shots were fired and no hardened villain expired before the footlights in melodramatic agony. 'Not a single dead body is found on the stage – death does not disfigure the stirring chapters of this wholesome romance.'[19]

After Daw quit in 1889, there followed a four year period of stagnation with a touring tragedian, Edmund Tearle, in charge. He was succeeded by Wallace Revill. This was not a good moment to take over the management of the Royal. Just across the road, in Tudor Street, there was a wooden structure known as the Grand Circus which had recently taken to presenting sensation plays and melodramas. Such competition, so close at hand, was alarming enough. Then, in 1893, the building was completely destroyed by fire and its owner, Alexander Stacey immediately set about replacing it with a traditional theatre. In August a foundation stone was laid by none other than Sir Augustus Harris, old 'Druriolanus' himself. 1893 was the year that Sheffield became a city and on Boxing Day, just five months later, the 'City Theatre' opened its doors for the first time.

Over at the Royal, Revill had done his best to make some improvements. He had redecorated the auditorium in cream, blue and pink and covered the seats in peacock blue plush. Above the proscenium a handsome pediment, with masks of tragedy and comedy, proclaimed 'Act well your part. There all the honour lies'.[20] The new season opened with *Jane Annie*, a comic opera which boasted a libretto by J M Barrie and Arthur Conan Doyle. But after that there were no great attractions and to make matters worse things got out of hand in the gallery:

> The performance took place in the auditorium instead of on the stage, and the members of the company were treated to a full and free exhibition of unchecked rowdyism. Jeers, shouting, mocking cries, cat-calls and swearing greeted the earnest efforts of a talented company of ladies and gentlemen....one of the performers had to come before the curtain and courteously appeal for a hearing. Mr Wallace Revill is new to the city, and is not yet acquainted with the ways of the Sheffield rough. We would advise him to procure the services of a dozen muscular "ejectors" for the rest of the week and distribute them among the "gods" in the upper circle and gallery.[21]

Sheffield may have been accorded a new civic dignity – but it did not take much for the 'gods' at the Royal to be as undignified as ever.

So, in 1893, the Theatre Royal, now over a hundred and thirty years old, reached another crossroads. The managers had constantly struggled to keep their heads above water and the success of Thomas Youdan's theatres had not helped. Dozens of music halls were now catering for the lower end of the market and many other places of entertainment had opened in the latter half of Victoria's reign. Yet the Royal was still there – and, indeed, would continue to entertain the people of Sheffield for another forty years.* Against all the odds it had somehow managed to retain its status as Sheffield's premier theatre.

Across the road the new theatre had opened and everything was about to change. Soon, nearby, there would be two large and very plush music halls, the Empire and the Hippodrome, which would not only see off many of the little music halls but also provide even more competition for Sheffield's oldest theatre.**

---

* The Royal was destroyed by fire in December 1935.
** The Empire opened on Charles Street in 1895. The Hippodrome opened on Cambridge Street in 1907.

The Adelphi – that place by the Cattle Market

On 23 April 1838, the Royal Amphitheatre opened on Blonk Street on a site backing onto the River Sheaf. Like Astley's Amphitheatre and the Surrey Theatre in London, it was a large building containing a circus ring and a proscenium stage. The aim was to provide a permanent home for circuses and equestrian entertainment. However, it soon proved impossible to keep going all the year round and the building often remained dark for many weeks. By 1844 the proprietors had had enough and put the building up for auction. The starting price was a mere £1,600 – just enough to pay off the outstanding mortgage. There were no bids.

Part of the problem was that the building lacked a clear identity for each new management seemed to think it needed a new name. Moffatt and Harmston, who ran a successful equestrian show, called it the 'Arena.' The Van Amburgh Company with its 'celebrated' lions, Mr Sweeney 'the famous Banjo Player' and Bolivar 'the Wonderful Performing Elephant', rechristened it the 'Circus and Theatre'.[*] For the best part of a decade it struggled to find a sense of direction. Then, in 1847, the lessee, Levi Brown Titus, obtained a theatre licence and his enterprising successor, John Woodward, set about converting the building to a more suitable home for drama. The stage was reconstructed and seating capacity was increased, using the old circus ring for stalls. The newly named 'Adelphi Theatre' was launched on 27 December.

To begin with Woodward played safe and settled for productions that would not make too many demands on the audience. There was a pantomime, *The Queen of the Shining River*, *Marie Mignot,* a French comedy, and a jolly romp called *The Eton Boy* in which a versatile young actress, Isabel Dickenson, played the dual roles of Tom, 'a regular rattler' and Fanny, 'a young lady rather refractory'. The *Independent* was often critical about productions at the Royal but it cared even less for those at the Adelphi – that theatre down by the Cattle Market. Even before the new theatre opened the paper had been unenthusiastic and wondered whether playgoers were likely to be advantaged by having two 'houses' open at the

---

[*] 'Circus and Theatre' was its working title when it was under construction.

34

same time. Now, although there was some praise for Isabel Dickenson, it was still not impressed and pronounced the Adelphi to be 'inefficient in the presentation of good plays.'[22]

Perhaps stung by this criticism Woodward brought in a tragedian, Thomas Lacy, to play the lead in two well-known serious dramas, Bulwer-Lytton's *Richlieu* and Sheridan Knowles' *The Hunchback.* But these heavier plays proved unpopular and were dropped by the end of January. So it was back to comic pieces with very low prices but this made little difference and, in March, Woodward cut his losses and booked Pablo Fanque's exciting equestrian show to round off the season.

Woodward gave up in June 1848 and Richard Cockrill took over for a few weeks. He opened with the return of Van Amburgh and his trained animals with Cockrill himself appearing as Hector Timid in *Morok, the Beast Tamer, the Dead Shot* − a 'new, grand, romantic spectacle.' Animal shows were always popular, and prices rose slightly but it was reported that the boxes remained almost empty while the gallery, still only threepence, was full to overflowing.

Van Amburgh brought his animals to the Adelphi

By July the animals had moved on and the Adelphi chalked up its first real success. Sarah Anderton, who a few months earlier had done well at the Royal, now came to the Adelphi to play the part of Mrs Haller in *The Stranger,* a play which had long been a favourite in Sheffield. The *Independent* came close to showing some enthusiasm for her performance noting that she had acquitted herself with much credit and was loudly called for at the conclusion of the play.' [23]

35

John Sloan returned to Sheffield and took over the Adelphi at the beginning of the winter season. When he had managed the Royal he had brought in big stars and he set about doing the same at the Adelphi. Mrs Fitzwilliam made a hugely successful return to Sheffield this time with the playwright and comic actor John Buckstone in his famous play *The Green Bushes*. They were followed by the international stars Madame Céline Céleste and Benjamin Webster.

Top names at the Adelphi

Fanny Fitzwilliam

John Buckstone

Benjamin Webster

Céline Céleste

Competition with the Royal intensified. The Adelphi's prices were always just a little lower and some attempt was made to pander to the taste of audiences who might be attracted by bargain prices. In came Mr Abel with his performing dogs and *The Battle of Waterloo* was revived.

36

Animals on Stage

Animals were often involved in entertaining the people of Sheffield. Obviously there were plenty of them to be found in the circuses and travelling menageries but quite a number seem to have found their way on to the stages of the mainstream theatres. When the newly opened Adelphi was struggling it brought in one of the Victorian period's most famous animal trainers – Van Amburgh, and his wild animals. This was much more than a run-of-the-mill circus act for their programme included *Morok the Beast Tamer, the Dead Shot,* an 'original romantic spectacle in two acts'. Animals were often rewarded with important roles and were given appropriate recognition. When Vienna, a 'highly trained steed', appeared at the Royal in *Peeping Tom, or Lady Godiva's Ride to Coventry* he got equal billing with the leading lady even though his task was possibly rather less arduous. There were 'horse operas' like *Fly* in which the star, Etna a 'wonderful horse helped by Miss Edith Sandford', thrilled the audience with his bravery. Honours were probably about even in *Mazeppa,* a popular old favourite in which an actor, male or female, raced around tied to the back of a pony. There were also companies that specialized in plays where animals played the leading roles. Howard and Gleave brought no fewer than seven thrillers to the Alexandra in which a variety of dogs were the main protagonists.

Dogs and horses were the most regular performers but, in 1855, a couple of elephants starred in *The Wise Elephants of the East* and *Slavery* at the Royal. (Did they have to strengthen the stage?) Their visit was not wholly successful for during the Thursday night the male elephant broke off his shackles and smashed his way out of his stable. Strong gates stopped him getting out of the stable yard but not before he had done a considerable amount of damage. Horses and dogs were probably a safer option.

As shows became increasingly elaborate it was not unusual for animals to be used to 'dress the set' – living properties brought in to enhance the spectacular scenic effects. When the impresario Augustus Harris brought a racing melodrama, *A Run of Luck*, to the Royal, huge crowds gathered to see dogs and racehorses exercising on the streets. The show sold out in no time – almost certainly because of the excellent publicity the animals provided.

An unexpected success was Madame Warton's 'Celebrated and Original Walhalla Establishment' which pleased both the public and the critics:

ROYAL ADELPHI THEATRE
SHEFFIELD

UNEQUALLED Attraction!! Madame WARTON'S Celebrated and Original WALHALLA ESTABLISHMENT, from London for a limited number of Performances. Madame Warton will have the honour of appearing in her inimitable and original Personations of "Venus," "Sappho," "Innocence," "Diana," "The Lute Player," and "Lady Godiva " as represented by her at the Coventry Ancient Pageantry, on the 20th of June last, amidst the acclamations of delighted thousands; and will appear with her talented Troupe of MALE and FEMALE ARTISTES in their classic tableau vivants, introducing all the most favourite Productions of a Grecian Harvest Home – the Combat between "Idas and Apolla," "Venus Rising from the Sea" &c. &c. This splendid Entertainment was exhibited for upwards of 2000 successive representations, at the Walhalla, Leicester Square, London, and pronounced by the London and Provincial Press to be the most Unique and Classic Production of this country. The first performance will take place on MONDAY Dec. 11th, and every Evening during the Week.

Doors open at Half Past Seven; Performance to commence at Eight. Boxes, 2s.; Pit, 1s.; Gal.,6d. No Half Price to any part of the House

The man from the *Independent* was quite excited:

Madame Warton and her company have performed during the week with great applause. The limits of an ordinary notice would not contain a description of a tithe of the beautiful effects which have been exhibited. The *poses plastiques* are, in fact, illustrations of some of the finest works of art. They are living pictures and breathing statues. Several of the figures are extremely graceful and symmetrical, and others are admirable for well-proportioned developments of muscular strength.[24]

This was in fact a typical music hall act and there is little doubt that, in order to survive, the new theatre had to bring in popular entertainments as well as straight plays – and a few *'poses plastiques'* did no harm at all. But the new theatre was soon in serious trouble once again. Even a successful performance by the infant prodigy, Miss Kate

38

Ranoe, 'a mere child in years' did not help much.   And to make matters worse, audiences seem to have been completely out of control:

> Scenes of disorder nightly occur at the Adelphi Theatre of such a character as to call for the interference of the Bench. It was stated that, from the lowness of prices, the place was nightly crowded, chiefly with youths of both sexes, and the most demoralising effects must be expected to follow, as they mixed with thieves, prostitutes and the worst of characters. The disturbances which occurred in the gallery almost every night were such as to put a stop to the performances, and frequently three or four police officers had to be sent for to quell them. [25]

James Scott

Before the end of the 1848 winter season Sloan was bankrupt and for the time being that was the end of dramatic productions at the Adelphi. Although it had damaged the Royal, its few successes had not been sufficient to establish it as a viable competitor.   However, the Adelphi was by no means finished. Just under two years later, in February 1851, it was leased to James Scott of Manchester and the battle began all over again. Renamed the 'Royal Adelphi Parisian Promenade and Concert Hall' it was in fact little more than a very large music hall which attracted hundreds of pleasure seekers looking fo a good night out on the cheap.   But cheap beer and huge numbers soon kept the magistrates busy with cases involving all sorts of riotous behaviour.   Scot himself was directly involved in charges of assault and, perhaps more seriously, was in trouble for allowing dialogue on the stage without a licence – an infringement of the Theatres Act of 1843.

Charles Dillon, now back in charge at the Royal, saw this as a golden opportunity to undermine Scott. Appalled when he discovered that Scott's penalty had been a mere five pounds, he placed spies in the Adelphi audiences and threatened to report every infringement of the Act to the authorities.   But the magistrates had had enough and decided that the simplest solution was to grant Scott a stage play licence for three months on condition that he gave up his hugely profitable licence to sell beer. At a stroke they got rid of the Adelphi's boozy audiences and avoided being overwhelmed by Dillon's legal shenanigans.   Scott snapped up the offer and Sheffield once again had two theatres licensed to put on plays. The battle began all over again. Inevitably, prices dropped – and neither theatre prospered. Scott's licence was not renewed.

It is hard to see why but later that year the magistrates relented and decided to give the Adelphi another chance. Scott immediately went on the attack aiming to undermine Youdan, who was managing the Royal at the time, by changing the name of the Adelphi to the 'Theatre Royal, Cattlemarket' and plastering playbills with the new name all over town. Copies of some of these posters can be found in the corridors of the Sheffield Lyceum today.

The renaming of the Adelphi appears to have been born of desperation – a last ditch attempt to upstage the Royal. It failed and it was not long before Scott was in trouble once more. In July 1853, he spent thirty one days in prison and in September he was declared bankrupt with enormous debts totaling £1,600. So he left and the long-suffering proprietors of the Adelphi, anxious to rid themselves of this troublesome property, put the building up for sale once again. This time only one bid of £1,000 was received – and once more the theatre was withdrawn from the market.

Enter Mrs Scott

Amazingly, by October the Adelphi was back in business. The new lessee was none other than James Scott's mother, Mrs Elizabeth Scott. The old theatre, rechristened the 'Royal Adelphi', somehow managed to obtain a theatre licence and, with Scott effectively in charge once more, hostilities broke out all over again. Never one for half measures, he hired an army of bill stickers to paste his playbills over those of the Royal but the courts soon put a stop to that. It was all very silly.

When Mrs Scott's licence for the Adelphi came up for renewal it was refused. The Scotts did not give up but, unable to put on plays, they were forced to turn to acts without dialogue. The most successful of these was Ella and her circus ring:

> Ella, the American Wonder who, with her Etherian Troupe, will appear in the Magic Ring. This Entertainment surpasses anything ever witnessed in England. Instead of sawdust, the Arena is placed on the Stage and covered with Carpets of the Richest Velvet Pile. The Press pronounces Ella almost Supernatural and more like a Fairy than a human child as she dashes through Fifty Balloons.[26]

Although full prices were charged for this popular spectacle, Scott still wanted to run the Adelphi as a theatre but, after yet another unsuccessful

40

attempt to obtain a licence, he and his mother finally gave up and went back to Manchester and the theatre closed down once again.

It reopened two years later with none other than Charles Dillon, the newly appointed manager of the Royal as the lessee. He had had the bright idea that he could economise by using the same company at both theatres – but neither theatre prospered and Dillon soon gave up the Adelphi.

By October 1856, however, there was a new manager eager to compete for audiences. Having been let down by the proprietors at the Royal, John Coleman was now managing the Adelphi. He secured a drama licence, gave the place a face-lift and advertised it as a 'Magnificent Temple of the Drama'. He took steps to launder its reputation for unruly behaviour by making sure there would be a police presence to keep an eye on potential trouble-makers. But he then came up with the ridiculous idea that the best way to beat the Royal would be to present the same plays during the same week. The plan was bound to fail and both theatres continued to struggle for survival. Coleman did not renew his lease after Christmas and, despite attempts by Harry Vandenhoff and the resident company to keep things going, the Adelphi closed before the end of the season.

Coleman tried again in 1857. By now, Charles Webb was in charge at the Royal where the proprietors were suing both Dillon and Coleman. Stung by this, the two joined forces against what Coleman described as the 'common enemy' and Dillon cooperated in the running of the Adelphi. He brought in 'a Metropolitan Company formed expressly for the occasion' and delighted audiences with his performance as William, the patriotic British tar, in *Black Eyed Susan* and a number of other popular roles. But this joint venture also failed and on 13 November Coleman took a benefit – and left.

The Adelphi in Limbo

After this, the Adelphi remained dark until February 1859 when Huntley May, who had worked with Dillon at the Royal, decided to try his luck – and failed. A year later, Thomas Youdan took a long lease but it seems that even he was not quite sure what to do with this white elephant of a theatre. He opened it occasionally and there were rumours that he might turn it into an enormous concert hall – but it all came to nothing.

And so the Adelphi was now no more than a dilapidated storehouse. The proprietors of the Royal must have been delighted that, at least for the time being, that troublesome theatre down by the Cattle Market was no longer a threat.

Tommy Youdan and the Surrey in West Bar

*Youdan (centre) with members of his company the day after
fire had destroyed the Surrey Theatre*

The Surrey Music Hall

Thomas Youdan must be regarded as the most important figure on the
Sheffield theatrical scene during the Victorian period.   For more than a
quarter of a century he managed his theatres with flair and imagination. He
was a huge man with a huge personality – tough and ruthless, yet extremely
warm-hearted and generous. He proved able to recover from disaster, pick
up the pieces and move on.   He was a great manager – and he was a local
lad!

He was born in the village of Streetthorpe, near Doncaster, in 1816, and
began his working life as an agricultural labourer. At eighteen he moved to
Sheffield, not expecting to find its streets paved with gold, but shrewdly
imagining it offered better prospects in life than the humdrum routine of
work on a farm. He learnt the art of silver stamping and was employed by
several local firms, but he quickly realized that he would do much better if
he worked for himself.

Spink's Nest and the Royal Casino

At about the time that Charles Dillon took over the Royal, Youdan abandoned his regular job and ran a beerhouse in the Park District. Then he moved into the town and took over a public house in West Bar known as The Spink's Nest. Like many other pub managers he realized that by providing some entertainment to help the beer go down he could substantially improve his profits. So he added a singing and dancing room and The Spink's Nest was soon beginning to make serious money.

The business was going well but Youdan was far from satisfied. He invested some £1,700 on extensive alterations and decorations and on 7 April 1849 he reopened The Spink's Nest as Youdan's Royal Casino. It seated 1,500. Despite his failure to secure a wines-and-spirits licence, the Casino immediately became a huge success and Youdan's ambition to become a top theatre owner was off to a flying start. Artists came from severa major cities and in October he brought in Mr William Cox of London – an 'Unparalleled Attraction, Grand Combination of Novelty'. He was to 'appear every evening and exhibit his unrivalled Dissolving Views, Chromotopes, and Phantoscopes illuminated by the Oxy-Hydrogen Lime Lights and illustrated with Instrumental and Vocal Music.' The Grand Scenes included 'The Ship on Fire, The Eruption of Vesuvius, etc'. West Bar had never seen anything like it and no less than 10,000 people visited the Casino during Christmas week.

Respectability was all important and Youdan provided concerts of sacred music on Sunday evenings and he also realized that the name 'Casino' might be objectionable to influential puritanical elements in the town. So, in September 1850, the Casino became the Surrey Music Hall.

The Surrey Music Hall

The building's career as a music hall lasted thirteen years and during that time it had an eventful history. The new name added a touch of kudos for in London there was the famous South Bank theatre called the Surrey and Sheffield's first Lord Mayor was the Duke of Norfolk, Earl of Arundel and Surrey.[*] The building had been enlarged and now had a full stage and a tier

---

[*] Sheffield's long connection with the various Dukes of Norfolk can be seen in the two streets adjacent to the Theatre Royal – Norfolk Street and Arundel Street and just round the corner was Surrey Street!

of private boxes, with lower and upper galleries above and within a year, supported by his right hand man William Brittlebank, Youdan was able to make still further improvements. The Surrey became the largest public building in Sheffield, capable of holding at least four thousand people.

But that was not enough for Youdan. His applications for permission to present stage plays were repeatedly turned down unless he was prepared to surrender his beer licence. So he began to present plays as part of his music hall bill and, well able to afford the fines, he thumbed his nose at the authorities. In fact, it was not unusual for Youdan to find himself in the Magistrates' Court. He was sued by Mrs Montgomery, a singer from Manchester, for sacking her when she refused to dance in the ballet, 'Mad as a March Hare. ' She argued that her £3 a week fee was only for singing. The fine was loss of salary – plus costs. [*] He was also fined ten shillings for assaulting Henry Fulford, one of his singers, when he discovered him drinking in the White Swan between performances. But he was cleared of charges brought by Charles Parkin, a scissor-smith. Parkin and some of his rowdy friends had infringed the strict rules of the house – 'No whistling, shouting or stamping of feet or low language allowed' – and had been forcibly removed from their box. And Nicolo Deulin, a comedian, also failed in his bid for compensation after Youdan had pinned him to the wall in response to a claim for the cost of properties. Yet Youdan was justifiably proud of the way he ran the Surrey. His posters claimed that 'The unparalleled novelty and variety together with THE STRICT ORDER MAINTAINED at the above elegant establishment, nightly elicits the admiration of its numerous visitants'.

Although there was always plenty of singing and dancing at the Surrey, aerial acts were a great attraction with acrobats and trapeze artistes going through their routines some sixty feet above the audience. A typical week in December 1851 included the Brothers, Jean and Edouard Bouteiller – Italian Wonders 'whose Classic Evolutions and Picturesque Positions of Peril on the Double Corde Volante has caused the greatest excitement ever known in Sheffield.' It was also announced that Madame Lauretta would 'ascend upon a portion of the Atlantic Telegraph Wire from the Stage to the Upper Tier of Galleries'. Inevitably there were accidents. The stunt performed by another high-wire performer, Madame Salvi, was particularly dangerous. She too walked the length of a narrow wire from the stage to the top gallery

---

[*] All members of the profession were entitled to this.

45

but with added variations including a wheelbarrow. One night the wire broke when she was twenty to thirty feet from the floor and Madame and her wheelbarrow came crashing down. Amazingly no one in the audience was hurt but poor Salvi suffered serious injuries.

Nothing but the best – the Surrey is transformed

In September 1858, the new season saw the Surrey reopen with a great flourish after yet another major reconstruction. Youdan said that he had tried, for many years and at a great outlay, to make it 'a place of rational, healthy and intellectual enjoyment, unequalled out of the Metropolis for capacity, elegant in construction, and affording a diversity of amusement of a high order, which, it is hoped, will always merit large and respectable audiences'. The interior had once again been improved and enlarged. The centre of the new proscenium was adorned with a large clock 'made specially by Mr Holden of Fargate', surmounted by the royal crown and supported on either side by the arms of the Sheffield Cutlers Company and Sheffield Corporation.

By this time his resident scenic artist was William Ramsden, a first class painter who had previously worked in London at the Royal Lyceum Theatre. Ramsden re-painted all the scenery and was responsible for much of the highly elaborate interior decoration, modelled after the style of the new Royal Italian Opera House, Covent Garden.[*] The decor was white and gold on a crimson ground and an enormous looking-glass curtain covered the front of the stage reflecting the audience and the interior of the hall. The ceiling was decorated with allegorical subjects including Cupid's Triumph of Love, Flora at Play with Cupid, and the Marriage of Vulcan. Fifteen crystal chandeliers were installed with a total of a hundred and fifty lights. The centrepiece weighed half a ton with ten massive branches. The refurbished building also housed a new museum, a ballroom, a cosmorama and a picture gallery. The main entrance was in West Bar. Another entrance to the promenade and pit opened onto Workhouse Lane. Within a few years the Surrey had become much more than a music hall – it was in effect a highly successful Victorian leisure complex.

---

[*] Ramsden moved to the Royal the following year – but it was Youdan who brought him to Sheffield.

The opening night of such a magnificent building called for something very special and Youdan announced that on 18 September 1858 there was to be 'A Grand Concert of vocal and orchestral music'– with a printed programme, still something of a rarity in Sheffield. The star singer Madame Marietta was supported by a huge choir and a fourteen piece orchestra. Dancing was provided by Mrs William Ramsden, who, along with her talented daughters, was the favourite danseuse throughout the life of the Surrey. Prices were remarkably low. Private boxes cost one shilling, boxes sixpence, promenade four pence and the second promenade and pit three pence.

But all was not plain sailing. Only three days after the grand opening a flash and the sound of a pistol shot in the lower gallery caused a minor panic. Then, just when Youdan had more or less calmed things down, there was a shout of 'fire!'. At this the audience of over two thousand began to run in all directions. Once again Youdan tried to regain a measure of control but this time all in vain. One young man died when he threw himself through a window and four other people were trampled to death in the rush for the exits.

And there were some who sneered at this new place of entertainment:

Among ham and beef shops, oyster shops, and cigar divans, next door to a pawnbroker's and at the corner of Workhouse Lane, in West Bar, is the establishment thus eulogised. Like Holder's Music Hall at Birmingham, from small beginnings the proprietor, Mr Youdan, by getting the favour of the working men, has been enabled, with the result of their patronage, to erect this building, capable of accommodating 4,000 people. On payment of 6d, the visitor is free to boxes, pit, museums under the pit, and dancing room under the stage; 4d admitting him only to the gallery. Entering a lofty saloon, on one side of which is a large gaudy refreshment stall and tavern bar, we find our way into the so-called music-hall, which in construction, is a theatre. It is crammed full of an audience of men, women and children, enveloped in a stifling haze of tobacco smoke. We should have been glad to have found a higher class of entertainment than that afforded by the bill of fare – 'A female Blondin, double trapeze, globe perche, barrel dancer and clown, highly trained dogs, bottle and hair performer, tight rope dancing, negro vocalist, and Paddy Carey in Irish character'. [*]

---

[*] From an article in *The Builder* 5, October 1861, 'A further review of blots on Sheffield'.

Even Tommy Youdan could not please everyone!

Nevertheless the *Independent* was full of enthusiasm for the 'Museum of Curiosities'. 'The Museum, when re-opened, will be an attractive item in the programme, containing, as it does, a collection of trophies, minerals, fossils, animals, works of art, mechanical figures, etc. etc.'[27] It seems likely that there was in fact a small zoo for two years earlier Youdan had bought a number of live animals including:

a pair of Swedish wolves (nineteen guineas),
a Russian bear (eleven guineas),
some Eskimo dogs (seven guineas),
a cockatoo and cage (four pounds),
Cantelo's patent incubator or egg hatching machine (five pounds ten shillings)
and a Swedish brown bear (twenty five guineas).

This collection cost Youdan the equivalent of several thousand pounds at today's values – and, typical of Youdan who liked to do everything on a grand scale, the Swedish bear was said to be the largest in England at the time.[*]

An enormous cake causes problems

Youdan was a generous man who gave a great deal to charity – always making sure that his generous acts were well publicised. Unfortunately, one massive publicity stunt got him into serious trouble. For some time, Youdan had ordered a giant 'Twelfth Cake' for display at the music hall on 6 January – Old Christmas Day. This weighed four and a half tons, stood nine feet high and had a circumference of twenty seven feet. It was made by Mr Bassett, the Sheffield confectioner, and was taken to the Surrey in three drays drawn by two horses.[**] The cake was exhibited for several weeks and children from the National and Free Schools were admitted free of charge to see it. Eventually the cake was cut and sold at one shilling and sixpence per pound. There were tokens cooked in the cake and these entitled winners to valuable prizes. In addition customers at the music hall were given numbered slips of paper – and the lucky ones won a small cake. It all seems to have been perfectly harmless but in January 1858, the Magistrates found Youdan

---

[*] Youdan bought these animals at a sale at Wingerworth Hall in Derbyshire in April 1856 – recorded in *The Sheffield History Reporter,* March/April 1996.
[**] George Bassett , of ' Liquorice Allsorts' fame founded his confectionary firm in 1842.

guilty of breaching the Lotteries Act and sentenced him to seven days hard labour in the Wakefield House of Correction.

This probably gave satisfaction in some quarters, but a great many others were up in arms. A petition was immediately organised and an appeal launched. This was rejected by the Court of Queen's Bench and the sentence was confirmed, but Youdan's supporters were not going to give up. A public meeting was called to support a petition with several thousand names for presentation to the Home Secretary. In fact, word had already come from London that a pardon had been granted but Youdan, ever the showman, arranged for the news to be held back until the meeting was well under way. He then made a dramatic entrance and handed a telegram to the chairman, who very deliberately read the message: 'I have obtained the Queen's pardon. Stop the meeting at all costs'.[28] Tommy Youdan's standing in Sheffield had never been so high. But there were no more monster Twelfth Cakes.

Youdan struggles for a drama licence

Although The Surrey went from strength to strength as a music hall, Youdan still hankered after a drama licence. In 1857 he had taken a chance and arranged with Charles Dillon to stage *Othello*. News of this came to the ears of Edwin Unwin, a lawyer acting for the proprietors of the Theatre Royal who threatened to inform against Youdan and every member of the cast. It was calculated that this would result in huge fines of £160 each night so instead Dillon gave a free reading of the play, filling the Surrey and leaving many hundreds unable to get in.

Finally, much to Youdan's delight a drama licence was granted in 1863. By now, he had invested over £25,000 in his 3,000-seater theatre and had provided a spacious refreshment room inside the building This compared favourably with the Royal where people had go out for refreshments causing unwelcome inconvenience to passers-by. This time, therefore, there was a change of heart and Youdan's application was supported by nearly all the members of the Town Council as well as a few influential magistrates. On the understanding that he would give up selling beer, would not apply for a spirits licence, and would close his dancing rooms, Youdan was awarded a stage play licence for six months. At last he was the proud owner of a large, well appointed theatre which, given his popularity in the town, seemed certain to succeed. A final music hall performance was presented on

Saturday 26 September 1863 and the Surrey Music Hall re-opened as the Surrey Theatre just two days later.

GARRICK TAVERN,
SYCAMORE STREET.

RICHARD PILLEY takes the present opportunity of returning his sincere thanks to his Friends for the liberal support which has been conferred upon him since he took to the above Establishment; and hopes by paying strict attention to the wishes of his Customers, to receive a further continuance of their favours, to merit which will be his greatest study.

As the Theatrical season has now commenced, R. PILLEY has laid in a Stock of first-rate WINES, SPIRITS, BEER, &c., which he can with confidence recommend to those Parties frequenting the Theatre. He will also supply HAM SANDWICHES, on the shortest notice.

☞ Good and well-aired BEDS.

Audiences at the Royal had to leave the theatre if they fancied a drink. Youdan provided a refreshment room.

The Surrey Theatre – a major playhouse in West Bar

The year 1863 marked the start of a new era. Thomas Youdan had at last become the proprietor of a legitimate theatre and was intent not only on competing with the Theatre Royal in the field of quality entertainment but also on becoming a respected figure in theatrical circles. He prudently closed his bars and maintained his policy of no pass-out checks, so there could be no nipping out for a drink. The large bar at the front of the building became the picture gallery. But he wisely maintained his low music hall prices and the programme allowed time for two full productions.

Youdan's first season could hardly have made a better start. Hundreds failed to get in for *The Ticket-of-Leave Man* when the theatre opened on 28 September. The new company was led by the popular London actor Sam Emery as Hawkshaw the detective and included Emily Forde, an actress poached from the Theatre Royal. Then, in November, patrons were treated to their first taste of Shakespeare when Henry Loraine, billed as 'the great tragedian' graced the stage followed by a second 'great tragedian', Thomas Swinbourne. To guarantee that his first pantomime would be a spectacular success, Youdan acquired land at the rear of the building and extended the stage to a depth of 42 feet. *Sinbad the Sailor* opened on Christmas Eve and ran triumphantly for 51 nights. Each performance included songs by Maurice De Solla, 'the Great Tenor' and, inevitably, Mrs Ramsden's popular skipping-rope dance.

Sam Emery

Emma Robbarts

Before long, competition with the Theatre Royal intensified. Youdan scored a hit with a local drama by Henry Leslie, *The Trail of Sin, or The House of Bardsley, a Tale of Old Sheffield.* Audiences were delighted by some splendid new scenery depicting local landmarks such as Lady's Bridge, Middlewood Hall and Roche Abbey by moonlight. New actors at the Surrey included Emma Robbards, 'a leading lady of the Royal Surrey Theatre,

51

London,' Henry Leigh and J H Doyne. The most popular play of the season, however, was the first performance in Sheffield of *Faust and Marguerite,* Dion Boucicault's version of the Faust legend.

Triumph and Disaster

The enormous well-equipped theatre was still not big enough for the ambitious Tommy Youdan and he further extended the stage to a depth of 65 feet, installed additional seating and converted a former ground floor bar to a concert room.

Having secured a renewal of his licence, he now began to cultivate his social aspirations. One of the highlights of the 1864 season was a Grand Fashionable Night under the 'very distinguished patronage of Colonel Oakes, commanding the Troops of the Garrison and the 11th Royal Lancers, and the Officers of the 12th Royal Lancers and the Officers of the Buffs'. A splendid military band opened the proceedings followed by *The Duke's Motto,* in which Henry Loraine appeared in three roles, the third act of *The School for Scandal* and David Garrick's version of *The Taming of the Shrew* with Marie Wilton. But Youdan's crowning achievement was the acceptance by the Lord Mayor of an invitation to attend a performance of *The Merchant of Venice* on 27 November – an unheard of honour for an establishment in West Bar.

Marie Wilton

Sadly these triumphs were short-lived. Encouraged by his success, Tommy Youdan felt it was time to stage something really spectacular and early in 1865 he decided to impress his public with a new production of *The Streets of London,* a French sensation drama, adapted from the original by Dion Boucicault. Youdan was sure it would be a huge success even though it was an expensive production requiring

52

a number of extremely elaborate sets. The high point of the drama would be an exciting conflagration scene which demanded careful planning and a high degree of technical expertise. Henry Loraine was engaged for the part of Badger, the hero, together with the popular comedienne Jenny Willmore.

The Surrey was closed for two weeks to prepare but even so the play opened two days late, on 13 March 1865. Youdan had plastered the town with his bills. The house was full for every performance and no one was disappointed. As the climax approached, the villain set fire to a house containing incriminating evidence and the front of the building was immediately enveloped in flames. While a team of firemen (complete with a property fire engine) began to douse the conflagration, Badger rushed into the burning house and staggered out with the all-important document. The audience went wild.

The Streets of London

But it was all too good to last. Two weeks later real disaster struck. After the performance Youdan and Brittlebank did their usual checks and left the theatre soon after midnight. About an hour later, the roof of the Surrey suddenly fell in and a great balloon of fire rapidly engulfed the building from end to end. There was no such thing as a municipal fire brigade and, although engines from the various fire insurance offices were soon on the scene, little could be done. The interior was full of highly inflammable materials and the theatre was a total loss.

The best that could be said was that there were no injuries and no loss of life but Youdan was devastated. His magnificent theatre was gone along with irreplaceable scenery, his props and valuable pictures and the contents of his museum. His financial loss was said to be £30,000, probably millions in today's terms, and the ruined building remained untouched for nearly ten years.[*] But this was Tommy Youdan and he still had the energy, the ambition and the imagination which previously had transformed a pub with a singing room into Sheffield's finest theatre. For him the solution was obvious. He had to begin all over again. So he did.

The Surrey was completely destroyed

---

[*] In 1875 the building was put up for auction but the highest bid was only £16,500 and it was withdrawn from sale. When it was eventually sold and redeveloped, part of the site was used for the construction of the New Vestry Hall, a sort of temperance music hall, which opened in 1881.

The Alexandra – a new life for the old Adelphi

In 1860, Youdan had taken a long lease on the dilapidated old Adelphi building.[*] Busy with other projects, he showed little enthusiasm for running a second theatre and the old building became no more than a store for scenery and paint. After the fire at the Surrey, however, it did not take him long to see the Adelphi as the perfect solution to his problems. But there was much to be done. He had little capital and the magistrates refused to give him a theatre licence. So he dusted down the old building, gave it a lick of paint and opened it as a music hall.

On 12 October 1865, just six months after the disaster at the Surrey, the Adelphi reopened as the 'Alexandra Music Hall'. It was a strange opening night for a music hall. There were no acrobats, no jugglers, no tight-rope walkers and no comedians. Instead there was a full scale performance of Handel's Oratorio *Judas Maccabeus* featuring the Sheffield Choral Union. The Union had quarrelled with the manager of Sheffield's only concert hall, the Music Hall on Surrey Street, and Youdan offered them the chance to perform, free of charge, in his hastily refurbished and very large theatre.

The *Independent* was full of praise:

> The liberality of Mr. Youdan in giving the committee the free use of the handsome hall, enabled them to give this oratorio at "People's Prices" and the attendance must have amply justified their expectations......The audience showed a keen appreciation of the performance, and the success of the entire performance was unmistakable. [29]

It was estimated that there were nearly three thousand in the audience, almost certainly a record for a classical concert.

The following night members of the Choral Union returned and performed as part of a music hall bill. Prices remained low – Private Boxes 2s, Amphitheatre 1s, Boxes 6d and Gallery 3d.[30] The Alexandra Music Hall could hardly have got off to a better start – and opening with a

---

[*] See page 41.

sacred oratorio did much to convince the town that the new theatre was in safe hands.

The Alexandra Opera House and Music Hall

Youdan was definitely back in business and by 1868 he had persuaded the magistrates to grant a theatrical licence. With this new status came a grand new name – 'The Alexandra Opera House and Music Hall', but it was popularly known as either 'The Alex' or 'Tommy's'.[*] Youdan ran his own stock company and signed up Oliver Cromwell, who had been at the Royal for many years, as wardrobe master and stage manager for Mrs Pitt. Cromwell was also a versatile actor who could turn his hand to writing when required. Once again Tommy Youdan's judgement was impeccable.

Sims Reeves and George Leybourne - two flamboyant characters at the Alex

Very often programmes at the new theatre combined popular drama with music hall acts and this proved to be a winning formula. There were also occasional concerts with high-class

---

[*] Nearly thirty years later Druriolanus, Augustus Harris, made a reference to 'Tommy's' when he laid the foundation stone for the City Theatre.

soloists such as the tenor Sims Reeves. Reeves was a true star, highly paid and with a temperament to match. He was known for his unpunctuality and seldom consented to sing an encore but he seemed more than happy with his reception at the Alexandra and not only turned up on time but also gave an encore, the ballad 'Come into the garden Maud.' It was not long before Charles Dillon came for a season of Shakespeare. Then came George Leybourne, 'Champagne Charlie', a music hall star with a personality to match that of the Alex's flamboyant owner. Leybourne brought a touch of class to Blonk Street when he arrived, like royalty, in a coach! Word soon got round and every night he was greeted at the stage door by dozens of excited fans. It was all rather splendid.

Infinite variety – dogs, horses and footballers

As well as eminent tragedians and outrageously flamboyant music hall stars, there were dogs and horses. Some companies that specialized in plays where animals played the leading role and Howard and Gleave brought no fewer than seven thrillers to the Alexandra in which a variety of dogs were the main protagonists. Horse opera was another popular form of animal entertainment and Henry Powell brought his famous horses, Black Bess and Saladin, to appear in *Mazeppa, or, The Wild Horse of Tartary*. This was a very dangerous extravaganza featuring a thrilling scene in which an actor, lying on his back, was tied to a galloping horse.[*] Another thrilling drama, *The Lightning's Flash,* included a 'Grand Sensation Scene of the burning Chapparel in which the Steeds Rush through the Flood of Flames'.

Football was becoming increasingly popular in Sheffield, much to the delight of Oliver Cromwell, an enthusiastic supporter and a player with the local Garrick Football Club. The previous year, Youdan, always keen to climb onto any bandwagon, had presented a football cup for a competition involving a dozen local teams.

Over at the Royal on 12 November 1869, *Lady Audley's Secret* headed

---

[*] Mazeppa was first performed in Sheffield in 1832. For details see *Georgian Theatre in Sheffield* p 108

Theatres and Football

Sheffield can with some justification claim to be the birthplace of modern football and right from the start the two main theatres were actively involved. The world's oldest football club, Sheffield F C, was founded in 1857, the first ever 'Derby' match between this club and Hallam FC took place in 1860 .

The Youdan Cup

Thomas Youdan, the owner of the Alexandra, a man who was always ready to find something to add to his considerable reputation, decided to sponsor a football competition.   In March 1867 he presented the winners with the first ever football trophy– the Youdan Cup.   Youdan was not one to do things by halves and so there was a second silver cup for the runners up. Today international youth teams compete in Sheffield for the 'Youdan Trophy'.

The Cromwell Cup

In February 1868 the Theatre Royal, not to be outdone, also presented a football trophy. It so happened that their stage manger, Oliver Cromwell, was a football enthusiast who played for the local Garrick Club. He set up a competition involving half a dozen local teams who competed for the 'Cromwell Cup'. It was won by a recently formed team known at that time as 'The Wednesday' – and Cromwell himself made the presentation to the winners on stage after a performance at the Royal.

The two major theatres' interest in football went far beyond the presentation of trophies. In 1886 a joint pantomime team in full costume played a match for charity at Bramall Lane in front of a crowd of just under twenty thousand. A year later because of the damage caused by the huge crowd, permission to play at the Lane was withheld. However, the Licensed Victuallers Benevolent Institution came to the rescue and sponsored a match which was played before a smaller, and better behaved, crowd at Sheaf House The pantomime team, which arrived by coach, included Dame Durdan (of the Alexandra) and Dame Crusoe (of the Royal) as well as a wolf, Man Friday, a policeman, a cannibal king and a couple of flunkeys. The Victuallers, dressed in their working clothes, wore shirt sleeves and barmans' aprons. During the match several lady 'artistes' wandered about in the crowd selling flowers and matches   – and a couple of them were heard to offer to be kissed for a shilling 'in aid of charity'. It must have been a wonderfully entertaining afternoon.   The match ended in an honourable two-all draw.

the bill for a 'Grand Fashionable Night' presentation given under the patronage of the sixteen teams of the Sheffield Football Association.

The 1872 season marked the first time that Sheffield audiences saw a black tragedian, Morgan Smith, performing 'white' roles in *The Merchant of Venice* and *Hamlet*. But the season was also memorable for a tragedy of another kind. The Alexandra's night-watchman Thomas Bradshaw attacked his wife with a poker and axe and then hung himself forty feet above the stage from the rope used for flying scenery. Mrs Bradshaw died in hospital a few days later. This was a sad story of a soldier, believed dead, returning from war to find that his wife had remarried. She gave up her second husband but Bradshaw was given to fits of violence and the reunion led to tragedy. Morbid curiosity packed the theatre to capacity for some time to come.

More often than not, however, an evening out at the Alex was great fun. The local press often tended to ignore much of what went on there but the following gives us some idea of the comic offerings:

All who relish a rollicking, side-splitting farce, should not omit seeing *The Artful Dodger* running this week at the Alexandra Opera House. Mr Mat Robson as the Artful Dodger, and Miss Kate Berham as Susan Smudge, are inimitable, and are well supported by the other members of the company. Another rich treat is afforded in Monsieur Garts, who plays the tin tea kettle and concertinas from the size of a shilling to a dinner plate, with really marvellous skill, imitating birds, beasts, church bells and even the human voice, with a fidelity which, had he lived two hundred years ago would have rendered him a likely candidate for the stake. Perhaps his most difficult feat was playing two concertinas at the same time, one in each hand which he did with the greatest skill. He won a triple recall, each time being received with tumultuous applause. Of the opening drama, *Happiness at Home*, we will only say that it has a hundred most dramatic incidents crowded into three acts, and in it people make nothing of walking from Paris to Baden Baden in half an hour, whilst ladies rush about the streets of London, morning and evening, in full dress, and the most wonderful single combats take place under Waterloo Bridge, over which the luxuriant foliage of forest trees droops gracefully. There is a lady in it who is continually appearing on the scene, taking the part of innocence against villainy, and

59

generally having a couple of pistols about her, which she is continually levelling against the same two men. The plot we will not attempt to give; but we confess that we should like to see the carte de visite of the author. We are convinced that he must be the most remarkable genius ever born.[31]

Brittlebank becomes the lessee

By December 1874, Youdan was beginning to feel the strain of his hectic life style. He transferred the lease of the theatre to his manager, William Brittlebank, and retired to his farm near Filey. He seemed to find it difficult to stay away, however, and a week seldom passed when he did not spend a day at the Alex. So, to begin with, Brittlebank made few changes and the theatre prospered. Audiences were fascinated by the latest technology and, in November 1875, they flocked to see *Across the Continent* in which disaster was averted by the timely arrival of soldiers, summoned by a message sent by the newly invented electric telegraph. To the delight of the packed houses one of these newfangled instruments was actually used on stage.

But a huge shock destroyed this sense of enthusiasm at the end of 1875 when the Alexandra narrowly escaped sharing the fate of the Surrey Theatre. Disaster struck during a performance of *Aladdin* on 28 December while a huge audience were captivated by a spectacular transformation scene. A gorgeous fairy landscape, with tropical plants and flowers and beautiful nymphs, was brilliantly lit by limelight but suddenly, as the set revolved, a gauze festoon caught on the petal of a flower and was thrown onto an unprotected gas jet in the wings. This caused a tremendous blaze in full view of the auditorium. Fortunately the frightened audience were able to leave safely through the emergency doors and the gauze burned out in a few seconds. As soon as the danger was over Oliver Cromwell brought on the harlequinade. There was a loud burst of music, everyone returned to their seats and the sprites resumed their performance. But a terrible price was paid. High above the stage two eighteen-year old nymphs, Alice Gregory and Alma Oldale, were strapped to metal supports and the burning gauze set fire to their dresses. Alma died of her injuries and Alice was seriously burned. At the inquest, held at the Myrtle Inn, Heeley, Oliver Cromwell confirmed that in future the gas jets would be protected. The coroner returned a verdict of Accidental Death but made a recommendation that 'all manufacturers of costumes and stage scenery should take measures to fire-proof their materials.'[32]

Sheffield Fair Week was in full swing in November 1876 when news came that Thomas Youdan had died at his home in Flotmanby, near Filey, aged sixty. For over twenty five years he had been the dominant personality in the Sheffield theatre world. His body was brought to Sheffield for burial in the General Cemetery and the Alexandra closed that night as a mark of respect.

Brittlebank had taken over the lease of the Alex in 1874 but for two years Youdan, who was still the proprietor, had cast his shadow over the mangement of the theatre and continued to influence matters of importance. At last, at the start of the 1877 season, Brittlebank was firmly in control but to begin with he changed very little. He shrewdly maintained Youdan's successful policies and made sure that he kept up his predecessor's charitable interest in the community.

A daring young lady on a flying trapeze

The spectacular display by Madame Sanyeah, the Flying Lady, reviewed in April 1879, was typical of the high standard of music hall turns at the Alex. Indeed these often proved more popular than the theatrical dramas they were supposed to be supporting.

Her magnificent figure displays immense strength, and she is as graceful in her movements as she is daring in the execution of her perilous performance. On the trapeze she is a clever and precise artiste, and after showing a number of difficult feats through that medium, she comes to the most sensational part of her programme. Hanging head downwards from the trapeze she holds in her teeth a couple of ropes in nooses, at the end of which are inserted a cross-bar. To this an ordinary sized man clings, and is supported by Madame Sanyeah, who also supports in each hand another man. This feat evoked loud applause from the large house, but was easy compared to two other things which followed. Again throwing herself backwards, she hung from the trapeze with the cross-bar depending from her teeth, whilst a man swung himself by a long trapeze from the other end of the house, and swung on the bar supported by the lady's teeth. The last feat roused the spectators to a great pitch of excitement. Coming to a platform erected at the opposite end of the house Madame

61

Sanyeah seized the trapeze and hanging from it by her teeth swung over the pit. Then jerking her body she began to turn, and for fully a minute she swung to and fro over the pit, hanging by her teeth from the revolving trapeze. She descended amid a storm of applause and was compelled to reappear and bow her acknowledgements to the admiring house.[33]

After all that it is hardly surprising that the rest of the review consisted of only a few lines on the play, H J Byron's *Blow for Blow*. Madame Sanyeah was a hard act to follow!

Opera at the 'Opera House'

Although the Alexandra styled itself an 'opera house', no opera companies came until Brittlebank engaged The Carl Rosa in 1879. He re-upholstered the box seats and laid on special trains from Chesterfield at one shilling and threepence return. But he was bitterly disappointed. Despite bargain prices, the pit and gallery regulars stayed away and the better seats failed to attract opera-lovers accustomed to the more gentile atmosphere of the Theatre Royal. Undeterred, just six weeks later, he jumped at the chance to bring The Carl Rosa back. This time business was much better – and a performance of *Mignon* sold out completely.[34]

From then on opera and operetta were to feature regularly at the Alexandra, with visits from no fewer than twenty companies. Carl Rosa proved to be the main attraction and it was performances of *The Bohemian Girl, Maritana* and *Faust* that topped the bill. There was a range of other choices, however – light operettas such as *The Rose of Castile* and *The Lily of Killarny,* more serious works such as *Il Trovatore, Fidelio* and *Carmen* and burlesques such as *Cruel Carmen or The Demented Dragoon and the Terrible Toreador.* Gilbert and Sullivan operas were not performed – D'Oyly Carte remained faithful to the Royal.

Now there was some evidence that Sheffield audiences were beginning to tire of sensation drama and turn to comedies and operatic productions. On 7 July 1880, a play called *Gain* drew rather smaller houses than usual and the man at the *Independent* was delighted:

Compared with the crowded houses which Mr Brittlebank has recently been having, the attendance last night at the Alexandra, although large, was not of the character which

62

really good plays collect. It clearly proved that plays of the sensational class are on the decline, at least in this town. Such plays as *The Flying Scud* and *New Babylon* are not appreciated by the general public as they were a few years since.[35]

Shakespeare was certainly not in decline. Several touring companies staged all the usual plays to appreciative audiences and leading roles were performed by some top class actors – even Barry Sullivan found his way down to Blonk Street. There were also some serious modern dramas. By 1880, Arthur Wing Pinero was fast developing a reputation as an important dramatist and in that year the Alexandra was the first Sheffield theatre to stage his *Hester's Mystery* and, in November, another Pinero play, *The Money Spinner,* did even better.

Lillie Langtry, now manageress of her own company, chose to make her first appearance in Sheffield at the Alex. Here was the 'Jersey Lily', a society lady, mistress of the Prince of Wales, performing at the Alexandra down by the Cattle Market! Most of the audience probably came out of curiosity but, although she was never regarded as an outstanding actress, she played Rosalind in *As You Like It* and Kate Hardcastle in *She Stoops to Conquer.* The *Independent*, following her first night on 11 July 1882, said that the theatre presented an altogether different appearance:

Lillie Langtry — famous or notorious?

The dress circle was full of ladies and gentlemen in evening dress, and though the pit – ever the backbone of a theatre and the most critical part of the audience – was as crowded as it usually is, the occupants of the gallery were conspicuous by their lessened numbers......Mrs Langtry was somewhat warmly received, and at the conclusion of the first act (the play was *An Unequal Match* by Tom Taylor) she was called before the curtain. This compliment was not repeated, but Mrs Langtry should not be alarmed thereby. Sheffield audiences are proverbially cold and undemonstrative but they are appreciative nevertheless.[36]

63

Langtry later performed at the Royal – but the Alex got in first!

The year 1883 saw the first of many visits to Sheffield by Wilson Barrett who chose the Alex for a two-week run of his London hit – *The Silver King* by Henry Arthur Jones and Henry Herman. The visit was a huge success and Barrett and *The Silver King* returned to the Alex many times.

Brittlebank breathes new life into an ageing theatre

By 1883, Brittlebank could at last see his way to a programme of modernisation. The stage badly needed to be enlarged but the theatre backed onto the River Sheaf. So what could be done? Brittlebank came up with the perfect solution. Cast iron piers were driven into the river bed enabling him to increase the depth of the stage area by 20 feet and create an extra 1,100 square feet of usable space.

A brand new hot water system was installed and backstage there were eight new dressing rooms and a number of lavatories. The enormous new scene painting workshop, 45 feet long by 14 feet wide, provided plenty of scope for the carpenters and gas fitters. There was a new stage door on Exchange Lane which also served as an additional safety exit and now all the backstage woodwork was treated with fire-proof asbestos paint. The changes to the auditorium were equally spectacular. It was repainted in pink, grey and gold with the ceilings and boxes decorated in Louis XIV style copied from the Tuilleries in Paris. The sides of the pit were crimson with a wide dado and border, harmonizing with the crimson seats and drapery in the boxes and dress circle.*

The stage was now one of the largest in the provinces. Pantomimes increased in scale and magnificence and famous touring companies were attracted by the high quality scenery produced by the workshops.

Although opera and operetta were now popular attractions, Brittlebank decided to drop 'Opera House' from his bill posters. In future his theatre would be advertised simply as 'The Alexandra'. By now his public knew, without reminding, that he could offer the same high quality productions as his old rival, the Theatre Royal.

In October, the Alex welcomed its first Drury Lane production – *Human Nature* by Henry Pettit and Augustus Harris, the great 'Druriolanus.' Harris's company brought all its own scenery, stage machinery and some extravagant special effects. There were battles between the English troops and the troops of the Mahdi in Sudan followed by a victory parade through Trafalgar Square. The audience cheered this amazing spectacle and within six months the drama was brought back for another week. This time over sixteen thousand tickets were sold.

The finest and largest theatre in Yorkshire

Brittlebank continued to make improvements to his theatre and in 1887 he boasted that the Alexandra was now 'the finest and largest theatre in Yorkshire'. He installed a new 'sun light' of 160 gas burners to replace the fifty year old gas chandelier. Once again the

---

* A detailed description of Brittlebank's improvements can be found in the *Independent* 11.9.1883.

Opera and operetta

There is little doubt that the Victorian period was opera's golden age. All over Europe crowds flocked to performances of Grand Opera and its near relatives Operetta and Opera Bouffe. What was its effect on Sheffield? In the early days opera's popularity was decidedly mixed. It did not begin well. In 1847 Charles Dillon brought a number of popular operas to the Theatre Royal which were performed by some of the top stars of the day – and they played to empty seats. The experiment was described as an 'unmitigated failure'. 'Sheffield....has not exhibited alacrity in support of attempts to improve the character of public entertainment …. To perform Grand Opera in an efficient manner on the Sheffield stage would require many months preparation'.

In the early fifties, Jenny Lind and other international opera stars gave concert performances at the Music Hall on Surrey Street. It is possible that they may have had some effect for when the First English Opera Company came to the Royal in 1853 'every part of the House was too small for the great numbers who applied for admission'. Soon the press were able to report that things were looking up and that audiences 'included some of the best families in the town and neighbourhood'.

So it took a while for Sheffielders to realize that they actually liked opera — but when they finally woke up they went for it in a big way. Between 1860 and 1870 just five companies came to Sheffield. In the next two decades at least thirty five different companies brought operas and operettas to the Royal.

However, support for opera tended to ebb and flow. For example The First English Opera Company (under a variety of names) continued to perform frequently in the fifties and sixties and must have found it worth their while. But when *The Grand Duchess* came to the Royal in 1868 and Sheffield had its first taste of Offenbach, the result was disappointing. Audiences were so small that the show was withdrawn — yet a few months later the same operetta attracted 'crowded houses and rapturous applause'. Similarly when William Brittlebank signed up The Carl Rosa Company and brought opera to the Alexandra for the first time, the visit was a complete failure. Yet, when he daringly brought them back just six weeks later, they were a big success.

Two companies stood out. The Carl Rosa Grand English Opera brought a mix of grand opera and operetta to the Royal on no fewer than ten occasions. But even they were overshadowed by Gilbert and Sullivan. Between 1878 and 1893 D'Oyly Carte's Savoy Operas were regular visitors and it was not unusual for them to come to the Royal on two, three and sometimes even four occasions in single year. By far Sheffield's favourite 'grand' opera was *Maritana* an English work dating from the 1840s. Two other early works, *The Bohemian Girl*, another English opera, and Bellini's *La Sonnambula* were also extremely popular and there were frequent performances of *Il Trovatore* , *Faust*, *The Rose of Castile*, *Norma* and *Don Giovanni*.

66

auditorium was re-gilded and re-painted and there was a new actdrop, designed by the theatre's resident scenic artist William Maugham and his son Percy, which showed the ruins of the Temple of Jupiter surrounded by white satin and crimson painted drapery. The building could now accommodate an audience of 3,400 – considerably more than the 2,900 at the Royal. It is worth remembering that, although these figures included a few hundred standing places, today the current combined capacity of Sheffield's two main theatres, the Crucible and Lyceum, is only around a couple of thousand seats.

When smallpox brought an early end to both the big pantomimes in 1888, the loss of these reliable money-spinners was a serious blow. However, by March, after a thorough cleansing, the Alex was ready to welcome the return of Wilson Barrett. This time he brought his latest production, *The Golden Ladder.* This had all the characteristics of a standard Victorian melodrama, but the *Independent* nevertheless saw it in a favourable light:

> To those playgoers whose predilections lie in the direction of melodrama – we now refer to the healthy, latter-day melodrama, not to the old blood and thunder, pistols and policemen school of plays – his name (Barrett's) is a tower of strength, for he was one of the first to raise melodrama from its sensational, inartistic surroundings and place it on the footing it now occupies...... The incidents are led up to and emphasised in dialogue of exceptional excellence. Respecting the representation of the piece last night nothing but unqualified praise can be bestowed. A more uniformly excellent company has never previously been seen in melodrama in the provinces.[37]

Sheffield's love affair with Wilson Barrett was set to continue for several years – though in 1893 he blotted his copybook. During a long-running dispute between employers and coal miners, he showed he was not afraid to wade into local politics. In one of his regular curtain speeches, he referred to the considerable hardship being endured by the miners and their families and said that it seemed

Wilson Barrett

67

strange that in the nineteenth century such a dispute could not be settled without causing so much suffering. He hoped that 'he might prove a mascot to bring good luck', and that 'the dispute might be at an end before he quit the town'. Barrett faced considerable criticism for meddling in local affairs but in a long interview with the *Independent* he maintained that he had as much right as anyone to speak his mind from the stage.[38] At the end of the week he gave five hundred loaves of bread for distribution among the strikers – and Brittlebank added a further three hundred.

Enthusiasm for Shakespeare – but prices go up

The Alexandra continued to go from strength to strength. By 1889, music hall turns were a thing of the past and the second plays which traditionally followed the main performance were now a rarity. Productions were of a high standard and even when one of the old pot-boiler sensation dramas turned up, it could now be staged with better scenery.

Osmund Tearle, a tragedian like his brother Edmund, came to the Alex in 1890 and his visit demonstrated just how much things had changed. His company performed a number of Shakespeare's tragedies to large and very appreciative audiences. The *Independent* was driven to ask:

> Who was it said that Shakespeare spelt ruin? Our working classes we have generally credited with a hankering after the weird, the stirring, murdering melodrama or the screaming, outrageous burlesque. And yet, last night at the Alexandra Theatre, was the pit and gallery crowded with the horny-handed sons of toil, as they so dearly love to hear themselves called, following keenly and appreciatively the most deep of the world's many plays – Shakespeare's *Hamlet*.[39]

In fact this was the third production of the play in less than a year!

But costs had risen, largely because of the demands of the increasing number of touring companies for ever more elaborate scenery, and after the midsummer clean-up Brittlebank increased his prices. Even then the top price was only two shillings and sixpence for the best seats in the dress circle, sixpence in the pit and fourpence in the gallery. There were no orchestra stalls in the pit which remained an area of un-numbered benches. Brittlebank also maintained the 'early doors' system. This allowed those patrons of the pit and gallery, who were prepared to pay an extra sixpence, to grab the best seats before the official opening time.

1893 marked an important theatrical event for the Alexandra – the first performance of a play by Oscar Wilde, straight after its successful inaugural run at London's Haymarket.[40] *A Woman of No Importance* opened in London in April – Brittlebank moved fast and brought Beerbohm Tree's production to his theatre in August. The *Independent* was most impressed:

> In so soon securing Mr Tree's provincial company, Mr Brittlebank, the proprietor of this house, has scored well. *A Woman of No Importance* has told her harrowing tale of outraged love and blighted hope to more critical audiences than that assembled at the Alexandra last evening, but hardly to a more appreciative one..... when it was at its height, a drop of a pin could have been heard.[41]

This was Brittlebank's crowning achievement as his theatre rose to the peak of its success. Despite the sneers of the local press and the accusations of vulgarity, the Alexandra, and before it the Surrey, had done well. Somehow the constant problems which beset the Royal did not seem to loom as large down in Blonk Street. Perhaps the key was that both Youdan and Brittlebank were in full control of their theatres. There was no board of proprietors and, importantly, no fluctuating (and often exorbitant) rent to pay. Both made a lot of sensible decisions, both had a care for the concerns of the local community and both showed a passionate commitment to the theatres in their charge. Above all they displayed a clear understanding of what the people of Sheffield wanted to see and did their best to provide it.

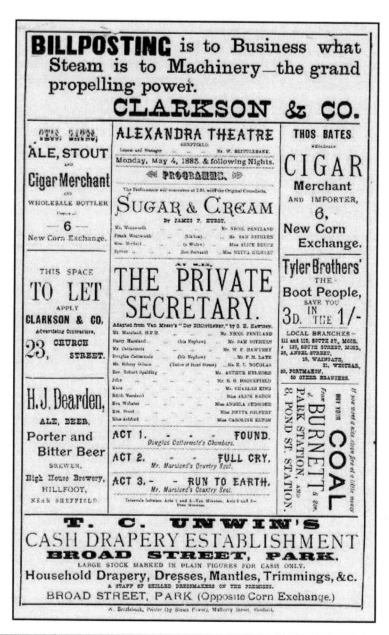

Alexandra Playbill 1885

Part 2
The Music Halls

The Earliest Halls and the West Bar District

More often than not it was the overcrowded, raucous, enthusiastic and volatile patrons of the gallery who helped to keep the major theatres afloat. They were thrilled by sensation dramas, they wept at the pathetic scenes of the sentimental plays, they laughed uproariously at the broad comedies – and to be fair – they turned up in huge numbers to catch a glimpse of the big stars. At the same time a large proportion of the fast growing population never even thought about going to the theatre. For them a good night out was to be found in the music halls.

Around the time Queen Victoria came to the throne, a new form of entertainment was developing. All over the country – especially in the industrial cities – inns and taverns increasingly began to provide musical turns for the paying customers. Soon some canny landlords realized that they were on to a good thing and set up special rooms where for a few pence people could drink and smoke – and listen to the songs of the day. 'Singing rooms', 'music rooms', 'song-and-supper rooms', 'free-and-easys' (there were many terms) began to emerge as something more than a sing-song at the end of the bar in a public house. As the century wore on a number of them would develop into minor playhouses and, indeed, one or two became very important theatres. From such small beginnings came the giant music halls of the 1890s and early twentieth century.

In Sheffield these small establishments provided a cheap night out for working class men (in the early days the patrons were mostly men) who lived in the densely packed streets of poor houses around local factories and workshops. The working day was long, street lighting was poor or non-existent and they did not want to venture far in the evening to find amusement. These halls had no need to advertise and a good many of them vanished without trace. But it was not too long before one or two felt able to make their presence felt.

Early Halls

The **Victoria Saloon,** attached to the Castle Inn on Snig Hill was the first music hall to advertise in the local press when in 1839 the proprietor, Mr J Hully, took space in the *Independent* to announce the opening of his saloon which was 'painted and ornamented in a far superior style to any other place of the kind out of the great Metropolis'. One of these places was possibly the **Bower Saloon** which was certainly up and running in January 1843 when it advertised a couple of dance acts.[*] In November 1845, it was announced that the Albert Rooms were to open at the **Falcon Inn**, Flat Street. The proprietor begged to inform his friends and the public that in addition to extensive alterations, he had, at considerable expense, installed a very powerful organ, and trusted that his arrangements would give 'general satisfaction to all parties visiting his place of amusement, it being on the London principle'[42]. Just a year later Mr B FitzPatrick, proprietor of the **Victoria Rooms** in Fargate, let it be known that his Harmonic Room would be open every evening at seven o'clock, where 'gentlemen will meet with amusement of first-rate order'.

So by the 1850s when the **London Concert Room** opened in Duke Street there was quite a choice of venues and a noticeable improvement in quality. The **Pheasant Inn Rooms** in the Park Area provided boxes, a pit and a gallery. It was, in fact, a theatre – there was even a 'grand fashionable day'.   Most establishments made their money from the sale of drinks but the Pheasant charged for entrance at one shilling, sixpence and threepence. Children were admitted to the boxes and pit for half-price.[43] The entertainment on offer in these early halls consisted mainly of vocalists, including comic singers. To begin with most halls would have employed local talent but it was not long before other performers began to appear – sometimes from as far afield as Scotland and Ireland.

Two Famous West Bar Halls

Although music halls began to spring up all over Sheffield, the greatest concentration was to be found around West Bar. Important among these were the **Britannia** and the **Gaiety**. Their premises were not completely demolished and parts of them were eventually incorporated in later buildings.[**] So we know quite a lot about the Britannia which started life in

---

[*] See Barker, Kathleen M D, *Dance and the Emerging Music Hall in the Provinces*, p33.

[**] We are extremely grateful to Andrew Woodfield for information about the Britannia. He and David Dawson, made an extensive survey of the converted building in 1972 when it was owned by William Green and Co, a firm who made and installed bathroom equipment. Andrew's help and advice has been invaluable.

a modest way in a room above the Old Tankard Inn but, around the height of the music hall boom in the 1850s and 1860s, developed into a full scale theatre[*]. A proscenium arch was installed with a decent forestage and wing space. There was provision for a front curtain, drop scenes and bars for trapeze acts and three dressing rooms. The ceiling of the auditorium was decorated with floral patterns and 49 mirrors framed in black and gold adorned the walls. Both the stalls and gallery bars were equipped with windows through which patrons could watch the show whilst enjoying their drinks and there was an area for dining.

In its early days the Britannia made its money by selling alcohol. Customers bought a token for threepence, presented it at the bar and were given a drink which was worth twopence. ^{**} By the 1880s, you could still get in for twopence although the best seats cost sixpence. Doors opened at six o'clock and the concert began at seven which allowed plenty of drinking time before the show started. Prices went up on special occasions. So, when 'Sir Roger', the notorious Tichborne Claimant, addressed his 'Supporters and Friends' in February 1885, admission prices were two shillings, one shilling, sixpence and threepence.

Popular turns included Little Nellie and sketch artistes Colvil and Edwards, 'negro comedians', Ted Jarratt's troupe of sketch artistes in 'Fracas', J M Jones' 'great pantomime company' and also 'The Mashers' Picnic' in which no fewer than twelve performers squeezed onto the small stage. And there was at least one really famous name associated with the Britannia – Dan Leno. He was probably the biggest star of late Victorian

Dan Leno

---

[*] It was certainly up and running in 1867 when the 'Tankard Tavern' was given planning permission for a new drain and gentlemen's urinal.
^{**} A few of these tokens still exist in private collections, stamped with the name of the hall – the 'Old Tankard Inn'.

music hall, quite as big in his own way as Henry Irving was in the theatre. Charles Dickens is said to have been impressed when in 1869 he saw young Leno, already a highly experienced nine year old, performing at the Britannia.

Some years later Leno returned to West Bar and in his autobiography *Dan Leno – Hys Booke, written by Himself* he tells his story:

We were engaged to appear at the Britannia Music Hall, Sheffield, and of course arrived on the Monday. Father and mother went to look for our lodgings and left me to get the luggage to the hall and prepare it for our performance in the evening. I went and borrowed a hand-cart, cabs were out of the question with us in those days, and after a good deal of exertion and deep thought, managed to take the things to the theatre, which I found in total darkness.

However, I put the baggage on the stage, except some costumes that I took upstairs to the dressing room. We were playing a sketch called 'Pongo the Monkey', in which we used our trick bedstead, and it was necessary to bore a hole in the stage in which to fix a strong wooden upright that formed the mainstay of the bed. I got the large auger we used for the purpose, but the hall was so dark that I couldn't see what I was doing, so I kept striking matches to look how I was getting on. After I had finished boring I went away to fetch something, and when I returned I was horrified to see a light shining through the hole I had bored. I guessed at once that I must have dropped a match through the hole and set the stage on fire.

There was not a moment to be lost. Off I dashed to the dressing room and seized a bucket of water. When I rushed back the light seemed brighter, and I did not waste a moment in pouring the water through the hole, and then waited with a beating heart to see the result. Had the whole theatre burst into flames I should not have been so astonished as I was for the result came in vocal form. A gruff voice under the stage exclaimed: "What ta devil is ta doin, oop thear?" Then there was the sound of hurried and heavy footsteps. I was always pretty nimble on my feet, but that time I think I beat all records. I shot out of the building before you could say James Brown.

From cautious and discreet enquiries I made afterwards I learned that underneath the stage was used by the proprietor as a stable for his pony, and the man who came to look after the animal had unfortunately placed himself in the best possible position for receiving my bucketful. It couldn't have gone better if it had been rehearsed for a fortnight.

Audiences

An evening out in Victorian Sheffield could be somewhat daunting. In the early days music hall audiences were largely all male affairs and most halls did not charge for admission but made their profits by selling alcohol. Obviously they would aim to sell as much as they could – with predictable results. As time went on things began to improve. The halls became more sophisticated and proprietors did their best to assert a measure of control. Notices began to go up – 'Women without escorts not admitted. No man admitted in cap and muffler'. At Thomas Youdan's huge Surrey Music Hall there was to be no 'whistling, shouting or stamping of feet or low language'.

The mainstream theatres had their problems too for they had the occupants of the gallery to cope with. It was by no means unusual for there to be empty spaces in the more expensive seats while the 'gods' were packed to the rafters. The manager would no doubt have preferred a more genteel, well behaved audience – but he often needed the revenue from the gallery to keep afloat.

The authorities were well aware of the need for strict control. In 1851, the manager at the Royal, Charles Dillon, found himself in trouble with the licensing authorities for failing to pay '£3 and £4 due for the attendance of the police at the Theatre'. It was pointed out to him that the Watch Committee 'only charged 1/6 a night for each policeman who attended'. Despite his insistence that he had been misled about these charges, Dillon was obliged to pay up. He was granted a licence 'on his entering into the usual sureties for the maintenance of good order'.

But the maintenance of good order was not always easy. The first night of the annual pantomime, normally on Boxing Day, could be a rather unpleasant experience.

….."boxing night" has (often) brought with it a crowd of persons besieging the doors without; and, within the theatre there has been a great noise, and a smell in which tobacco smoke, oranges, gin, and ginger-beer have appeared to be the prevailing ingredients. Then there has been a fight or two in the gallery and amongst its occupants we have usually had a conversation sometimes more amusing than polite; and the excessive heat has generally driven many to divest themselves of their coats, bonnets, and shawls. Besides all this, various interruptions to the performances are strenuously offered, and in spite of appeals from the manager, the piece which precedes the pantomime is invariably gone through in dumb show.

And Sheffield audiences seem to have been particularly difficult to control. In 1893, after a 'full and free exhibition of un-checked rowdyism' at the Royal, the local press noted that the current manager was new to the City and 'not yet acquainted with the ways of the Sheffield rough'. He was advised to bring in a dozen 'ejectors' and 'distribute them among the "gods" in the upper circle and gallery'.

76

Across the road from the Britannia stood the Gaiety. Until a few years ago bits of it could still be found in a building standing on the corner of Steelhouse Lane and Corporation Street, including the proscenium opening dressing romms and a handsome bar. It seated about 400 and like so many other music halls began life as the singing room of a tavern.

The Gaiety's most colourful owner was the German-born Louis Metzger, a pork butcher, who at one time had also kept the nearby Britannia. His shop stood next door to the Gaiety and there are many stories about Metzger's pet pig, who was apparently rather fond of beer. Metzger is said to have tried to keep his music hall select by charging sixpence admission instead of the more usual threepence and displaying the rather forbidding sign 'Women without escorts not admitted. No man admitted in cap and muffler.' The Gaiety closed in November 1893 when its current owner, Elizabeth Cromwell, went bankrupt. There were no bidders so the contents were sold off separately – a grand piano, 22 metal tables with marble tops, 9 wooden tables, 8 seats with upholstered backs and seats, 11 forms, about 380 wood and perforated stools, a stag's head, an aquarium, and a great quantity of glassware. It must have been an impressive establishment in its heyday.[44]

Other West Bar Halls

The **Black Swan** public house at the corner of Spring Street and Coulson Street changed its name several times during the late Victorian period. In the 1860s it reopened as the **West Bar Hall** and after that became the **Bijou Music Hall.** Towards the end of 1874 a new proprietor, Squint Milner, had the place redecorated and on 18 December reopened it as the **Star Music Hall.**[*] 'Comfortable and tastefully furnished' it was easily identified by the flaring gas jet in the shape of a star above the door. In 1887 an ambitious new owner, Alexander Stacey, remodelled and rechristened it as the '**New Grand Concert Hall (late Star)**'. It opened on Boxing Day, with a 'carefully selected Company of Star Artistes'. Although customers sat at public house tables or on benches, music hall style, it was not long before everyone was calling it 'The Grand Theatre'. Prices were fairly modest but by 1890, Stacey was able to splash out on further improvements. Three years later he became even more ambitious and opened the City Theatre in Tudor Street.

---

[*] Alfred 'Squint' Milner was quite a celebrity and was famous for his participation in long-distance races.

Building this new theatre required a good deal of capital so he sold his Grand Theatre to the brothers Edward and Oxford Weldon who transformed it inside and out, gave it a new plaster façade and yet another new name – this time the **Grand Theatre of Varieties**. The public house tables and benches disappeared and seating was redesigned on the lines of a conventional theatre to provide a greater capacity and a much greater income. The re-vamped hall was certainly impressive. The saloon had a large bar and was fitted up in the latest fashion – and the theatre itself fairly brimmed with technology. No fewer than forty electric lamps lit the stage and there was even a patent electric indicator to tell those at the bar which turn was performing.

The hall reopened at Easter 1893 and the man from the *Independent* went along on 4 April. He found it a 'pleasant, comfortable and prettily decorated place of amusement' and was particularly impressed by 'a very clever knock-about "Tandem Absurdity" by the Little Levite' and the 'exceptional success of Quinton Gibson as a female impersonator'. He does not say what he thought of 'Veda and Vera, Gymnasts and Champion Teeth Performers' or 'Burns and Leech, the Good Old Couple, Instrumentalists, Dancers and High Kickers' who were also on the bill. Doors opened at seven o'clock and the show began at half-past. Top artists such as the great pantomime star Billie Barlow and the vocal comedian Hiram Travers were engaged but by far the brightest star was Mr Charles Coborn, 'The Man Who Broke the Bank at Monte Carlo'. He had not appeared in Sheffield for several years and the local critics were pleased to see him return: 'His success is undeniable, and it is due in great part to the finished studies he has made of widely contrasting everyday people.'[45] Coborn was so popular that he was immediately booked to make a return visit in December.

For a while the Grand Theatre of Varieties did well but in 1895 it was forced to close by the opening of the mighty Moss Empire in Charles Street.[*] It was not on its own. New rigorous safety requirements meant that a good many smaller halls disappeared – and those that survived soon found themselves losing audiences to the luxurious Empire.

---

[*] It was given yet another face lift, some decent acts were brought in and twice-nightly performances introduced in attempt to draw people away from the plush Empire. Soon it was including moving pictures in its programmes and by 1909 it claimed to be the 'first all picture house in the City'.

Famous music hall acts at the Grand Theatre of Varieties — Billie Barlow and Charles Coborn

In Spring Street, just down the road from the Black Swan, were three other rather less pretentious halls. One was the **Punch Bowl** which Squint Milner took over in 1870. The new manager, J M Alleyne, who had previously run the Canterbury in Pinfold Street, brought with him an excellent picture gallery by 'the First Masters'.* Another hall in Spring Street, the **Blue Pig Concert Hall,** was no more than a public house with a singing room attached. The proprietor, Edward Parkin, occasionally organised small concerts with vocalists and pianists very similar to those found at the earliest music halls. There was some competition from the **Oxford Concert Hall** next door to the Blue Pig and in 1869 the two managements decided to merge to try to accommodate a single larger audience. But this arrangement did not last long and by June 1872 both little halls were back on the market.

The **Old London Apprentice Music Hall**, also known as the **London Apprentice** or the **London Music Hall** was taken over in the 1860s by William and George Cooper — father and son who later managed the **Royal Alhambra Music Hall** in Union Street.** Cooper Senior was very much a hands-on manager who liked to take an active part in performances occasionally leading the hall's small orchestra or taking on the role of chairman.*** Like Metzger he was keen to keep out the riff-raff and one of

---

* For information about the Canterbury see page 81.
** See also page 84.
*** The hall's regular chairman was a popular old clown called Jim Pymer.

the rules of the establishment was that no male was allowed to enter wearing a cap and muffler and no women without escorts or with a shawl over their heads. Admission was free. One of the London Apprentice's favourite vocalists was a local man, William Rowbotham, a grinder by profession with a splendid tenor voice. His engagement generally lasted three or four weeks and finished with a benefit for which he wore his grinders clothes.

When the Coopers moved on to the Royal Alhambra, the Old London Apprentice was thoroughly redecorated, repainted and cleansed before reopening under 'Mr W. Simpson, formerly of the Lyceum, Langsett Road'. After eleven years, the newly decorated and re-seated hall reopened as the **Hallamshire Hall** with a capacity of around six hundred. But it did not last long and in 1889 the building was advertised as suitable for Sunday and weeknight services. It became the 'Gospel Highway Mission' – a most inappropriate end for the Old London Apprentice Music Hall.

Yet another hall, **Wilson's Concert Hall**, stood half way along West Bar, attached to a public house. It opened in the late 1850s and remained in business for almost thirty years. A notice at the entrance warned: 'No Boys or Improper Characters Admitted'. Admission was charged at 'sixpence to the front seats and three pence at the back, money being returned in Refreshments of the Highest Quality'. In styling itself a 'concert hall' Wilson's obviously saw itself as classier than some other West Bar halls – and it was. An advertisement in the *Independent* of 26 February 1859 provides details of the night's bill:

> Mrs J.S.Cleveland, Mezzo Soprano Vocalist from the Edinburgh Concerts
> Mr H. Copeland, whom admiring audiences have pronounced the First Buffo Singer of the Day
> Miss Laura James, the Unparalleled Characteristic Singer and Danseuse
> Miss Milnes, in her Charming Ballads
> Mr J. S. Cleveland, Primo Tenor, from the principal Music Festivals
> Mr and Mrs Cleveland, who receive Rapturous Applause each evening in their beautiful Operatic Morceaux
> Leader, Mr T.S. Towndrow,
> Cornet, Mr Berrington, Piano-forte, Mr Goncanon
> Opening Chorus at Seven O'Clock

No jugglers, no acrobats, no comedians, no contortionists – this establishment was definitely up-market.

Sheffield's other Music Halls

Although many of Sheffield's music halls were located in West Bar,  plenty of other similar places sprang up all over town. There were free-and-easys, small establishments which usually had a more relaxed atmosphere than regular music and concert halls. The **Three Cranes** in Queen Street, claimed to be the original and oldest of these[*]. A typical poster for 5 November 1866 advertised it as a Free-and-Easy every Saturday and Monday evening at half-past seven, with 'Mr Doning as Chairman and Mr Backhouse as Vice-Chairman'. Located at the bottom of the Shambles another little hall, The **FitzAlan Room**, was well placed to attract crowds flocking to the two big Sheffield fairs. The public were urged to come and see

Bessie Bonehill

entertainments such as the 'Great French Giant for half-price'[46]. It would be nice to know exactly what the Great French Giant did. Did he sing, dance, tell jokes or play an instrument? Or did he merely stand around looking big? We will never know.

The **Canterbury Music Hall** stood in Pinfold Street just off Trippett Lane. It cost nothing to get in and the customers not only got a full music hall programme but could also visit its picture gallery[**] – all for the price of a pint or two. It is difficult to imagine how Sheffield's theatres and music halls would have managed without the ubiquitous Ramsden family. The resident violinist at the Canterbury was none other than young Master Ramsden, obviously following in the footsteps of his talented mother and sisters. The three Bonehill sisters, Marion, Bessie and La Petite played the hall in March 1870. Bessie, the most successful of the trio, became famous for her male impersonations and in 1884 she returned to Sheffield as principle boy in *Aladdin* at the Alexandra.

However, there seem to have been few other well-known performers and

---

[*] There is still a public house of that name on Queen Street.
[**] Arthur Williams, a former manager of Empire Theatre, writing in the *Independent* in 1927, highlights its picture gallery as its special feature.

in April 1870 the 'Canterbury Hall and dram shop' was advertised in the *Sheffield Telegraph* as being 'To Let, fully Licensed and Beautifully furnished'.

The **Fleur de Lis** in Angel Street which John Parsonage opened in the 1860s was taken over by his widow in 1869. When the site was swallowed up the following year by the building of Cockayne's, one of Sheffield's first department stores, she moved to the **Victoria Rooms**, a well established concert hall in Fargate[*] which claimed to have a more select clientele. The programmes, however, were far from select. They offered the usual fare of singers, dancers, comedians and speciality acts such as Mme Ohio, 'the Bearded Lady,' and Miss Florence Wriggbitte, 'the great Female Tenor.'

No one knows much about the **Underground Music Hall** and its location is something of a mystery.[**] In December 1883, *The Independent* announced the reopening of the hall after entire new decoration with a new star company and new management. But the advertisement gives no clue as to the location and no details about the performers. It merely informs us that 'the old Sheffield favourites, Chairman H Helliwell and Pianist J Sinclair' would be there.

In 1865, The **Union Music Hall** opened in Barkers Pool – opposite the site later occupied by the Albert Hall. It was only a small place but it was said to put on some good variety programmes. Admission was free, which suggests that the proprietor, like so many others, made his profit from selling beer. A bill for 1 February 1868 gives us a fair idea of the sort of programme we might have found in many of Sheffield's smaller halls –

> Annie Vernon, serio-comic and sentimental singer
> Nellie Edwards, infant serio-comique and clog dancer
> Tom Rushton, attractive serio-comic singer
> Harry Baldwin, great Cremorne comique and author
> Paddy Watts, the little Irish singer
> Mr Maurice, the Sheffield comique.

All washed down with a pint or two!

---

[*] The Victoria Rooms first opened in 1846 – see page 73.
[**] Bryen D Hillerby believes that it was to be found in the Wicker and cites the engagement of Edith Glynne at the high fee of £7.5s. for a week's engagement in 1882, the proprietor then being Thomas Machin. See Hillerby, Bryen D, *Lost Theatres of Sheffield* (Warncliffe Publishing) p 16.

Three Larger Halls

The **Union Street Assembly Rooms** opened in 1853 and eventually became the highly successful Royal Alhambra Music Hall. The Rooms stood at the corner of Union Street and Charles Street and soon became well known for panoramas – shows which, as sheets of canvas unrolled, transported audiences on thrilling trips to places that most people could only dream about.

Eliza crosses the ice in 'Uncle Tom's Cabin'

Exciting – and topical – was Pye's Grand Moving Panorama of 'Uncle Tom's Cabin with vocal and instrumental accompaniment'.* This was painted on several thousand square feet of canvas, with life size figures, 'the whole illustrating with truth and fidelity Mrs H B Stowe's world-renowned work.' A descriptive lecture accompanied the passing of the scenes. Batchelder's Panorama also had a six week run showing 'Dr Livingstone in Africa, the Indian Mutiny etc. With the Infant Sappho from London and instrumental music'. Tickets cost a fairly expensive one shilling, sixpence

and three pence – but panoramas provided an exciting and very enjoyable way for Victorians to keep up with world events. Lower prices were on offer to 'The Labouring Classes and Children'. The Rooms also offered attractions such as the celebrated mesmerist Captain Hudson who claimed many cures and was given a special dinner at the Cutlers' Hall by his admirers. Thiodan's Royal Allied Mechanical and Picturesque Theatre of Arts presented patrons at the Rooms with 'the World in Miniature' and even more exciting was a visit from Springthorpe who brought his 'Splendid Collection of Wax Work Figures, Grand Cosmoramic Views, Rock Harmonicon or Musical Stones, Mechanical Birds, Extraordinary War Horses, and Egyptian Mummies.'

---

* *Uncle Tom's Cabin* was published in book form in March 1852 and this show gave Sheffielders a chance to become acquainted with Mrs Beecher Stowe's sensational success.

Buoyed by the success of his six week run, Mr Batchelder decided to try his luck at management. On 21 November 1857, the Union Rooms reopened as the **Royal Victoria Concert Hall** – 'a First Class Concert Hall and Supper Rooms after the manner of Dr Johnson's in London'. Batchelder managed this first class establishment with his son, J Batchelder Junior, employed as pianist and musical director, providing 'First Class Vocal and Instrumental Music'. Since entrance cost a mere threepence which was 'returned in refreshments', it is hardly surprising that the Batchelders went bust. Eighteen months later the 'Union Rooms' were back on the market, offering 'one large room 24 yards long by 9 yards wide, and a suite of three smaller rooms, well lighted from the roof, suitable for a photographic artist or any light trade'. But it was not until March 1865 that the building reopened as the **Royal Alhambra Music Hall** with Edwin James Gascoigne as the proprietor.

Initially, Gascoigne employed Mr Alleyne as manager with Mr Chambers as Chairman and Miss C Chambers as an instrumentalist. Popular well-tried acts were engaged who appeared at other local halls such as The Britannia and The Surrey. By January 1867, however, Alleyne had moved on and Gascoigne found it impossible to attract a new manager. So, in June 1870, he reopened it himself as the **Royal Alhambra Concert Hall** with a 'grand array of talent'. The admission charge was fourpence. Business improved but not for long and once again the hall was forced to close. Determined not to give up, Gascoigne increased the capacity and reopened as the **Royal Alhambra Palace Concert Hall** on 23 December 1872. But all to no avail. In 1873 he went bankrupt and it was at this point that the hall was sold to William Cooper.

Cooper managed to rejuvenate the troubled theatre. He further increased capacity to around 2,000 and made various other improvements. The hall was entered from Charles Street by means of two staircases, one leading into the main part of the auditorium and the other to a horse-shoe shaped gallery supported on cast iron pillars beneath which was a long bar. The auditorium was decorated with 'several large and costly mirrors along the walls, of silvered glass and costing between eighty and ninety guineas each'. Seating was provided at tables before a large stage which had dressing rooms at the rear. Performers usually appeared twice during the evening for music hall audiences tended to come and go. Some clients would stay long enough to see all the acts and others just their favourites.

William Cooper had an original method of attracting people to the Alhambra. From time to time he would give Friday night Benefits when the holders of lucky tickets could win suites of furniture, tons of coal, bags of flour and other substantial prizes. He advertised by using a dray or wagonette to parade round the town accompanied by a brass band urging the public to join in the rush for tickets.

On Whit Monday, 1 June 1882, the building was completely destroyed by fire. Fortunately there was no loss of life or serious injury but the impressive company assembled for Whitsun week lost everything in the blaze. Mlle Franzini, lost her silver-plated bicycle, Harry Dale's thirteen silver bells were melted and the entire wardrobes of Miss Lizzie Villiers, Miss Rosa Blonde, Mr Dick Wadeson, and the 'negro duettists', the Brothers Ash, were completely destroyed. E S Drake, proprietor of the Grand Circus at the time, arranged for the Alhambra's performers to give a couple of benefit shows there to help them to recover their losses. Cooper, seriously underinsured, did not rebuild the hall and the site was redeveloped for shops and a hotel.

Unwelcome neighbours for the Royal

Right next door to the Theatre Royal was a disused carrier's warehouse and racket court. Thomas Jackson, a local man, saw the possibilities, took over the premises and transformed them into The **Royal Pavilion Music Hall.** The opening on 7 October 1867 received an editorial mention in the *Independent:*

> The Pavilion Music Hall: The new music hall, the Pavilion, next to the Theatre, was opened last night. It is a large commodious room, with galleries, is nicely decorated, and well lighted and ventilated. The internal fittings are not yet completed. From its central position this hall is likely to become a popular resort. The attractions are of the usual character.[47]

The proprietors of the Royal cannot have been pleased to have such a smart new neighbour.

The Pavilion was more up-market than many of its rivals in that it boasted a wine licence, possessed by few other music halls, but the programmes were much the same as those found elsewhere. They included Mrs Ramsden performing, yet again, her skipping-rope dance with her daughters Kate and Lily. One really big star to grace the stage of the

Pavilion was Jenny Hill, 'The Vital Spark' and 'Queen of Serio Comique Song.' *

Jennie Hill

Despite its wine licence and central situation, the Royal Pavilion did not prosper and closed in the late 1870s. The delighted management at the Royal seized the opportunity to acquire part of the site for a much needed enlargement of its refreshment bar and front-of-house facilities – and at the same time eliminate the possibility of further close competition.

Almost immediately, however, the Royal found that it had another unwelcome neighbour. The story of **The Grand Circus** began in 1879 when the 4th Yorks Artillery Volunteers gave up their drill ground and moved to a custom-built hall in Edmund Road. Charles Weldon snapped up the site – directly opposite the Theatre Royal – and built a large wooden structure to house a permanent circus. Previous attempts to provide Sheffield with a permanent circus venue had failed and this one was no exception. To begin with all went well. Weldon took over the reins himself and the novelty of the new building managed to fill the large auditorium for a few months. Then audiences began to dwindle and, in an attempt to make the building more versatile, the circus ring was boarded over to construct a conventional stage with an extra 400 seats, increasing capacity to about 3,000, suitable for use as a large music hall. But this was still not profitable and in February 1880 Weldon sold out to E S Drake.

Sunday Services for a Workmen's Mission

In addition to music hall acts, Drake was happy to let the Circus to anyone willing to pay. He advertised the building for 'meetings, lectures, concerts and Sunday services'. A leaflet by A S O Birch entitled 'Christian Work in the Grand Circus, Sheffield, being a Workmen's Mission to Workmen' pointed out that there were 100,000 workmen in Sheffield who attended no place of worship because they did not possess suitable clothes for churchgoing. A committee was formed to consider the problem and to decide whether to hire the Theatre Royal or the Grand Circus on Sunday afternoons. The Circus was chosen on the grounds that workmen would feel more comfortable there and this proved a popular decision. About 500 men

---

* Jenny Hill also appeared in pantomime at the Royal and performed at the Albert Hall – see page 124

attended on the first Sunday. A week later the number doubled and on the third Sunday 3,000 turned up. The capacity of the Circus was at last tested to its utmost extent.

During the week, a variety of music hall turns continued to appear at the Grand Circus with acts such as the Female Christys, clad in silver armour, who performed there in February 1880.[*] Princess Amazulu and her maids, her warriors and her medicine man also turned up having arrived by the Royal Mail steamer 'Nyanza'. They wore Zulu costume, sang a number of songs and choruses and performed dances said to 'defy description' and

PETER'S SIMPLE!!!
(A VERY SIMPLE YOUTH INDEED)

COMPOSED & SUNG NIGHTLY WITH UNBOUNDED APPLAUSE
HARRY LISTON.
IN HIS ENTERTAINMENT ENTITLED
"MERRY MOMENTS."

certainly must have been a hard act to follow! There were a few top liners including Dan Leno, by now one of the biggest music hall stars in the country and billed as the 'famous Irish comedian and champion clog dancer of the world.' Leno appeared with the 'Leno Trio' in their 'new sketch Pongo' in 1883. Other big names included W J Ashcroft, who sang Irish and patriotic songs, Harry Liston, famous for his *Merry Moments*, and George Leybourne, the original Champagne Charlie, who was so popular that hundreds were turned away each night.

Prices were very much higher than those to be found in West Bar − two shillings for a reserved cushioned chair, one shilling for a circle chair and sixpence for all other parts of the house. These prices did not include refreshments as the Grand Circus was not licensed but there were plenty of public houses in the immediate vicinity for those who wished to slip out for a drink. As well as music hall turns, the Circus promoted exhibitions of billiards and pyramids (a forerunner of snooker). Despite a rigid no smoking rule and prices ranging from one to five shillings, these displays proved immensely popular.

---

[*] Like many other groups of musicians and comedians, these ladies stole the name of the famous and highly successful Christy Minstrels. They also appeared at the Music Hall in Surrey Street and the Albert Hall– see pages 103 and 117.

'Leno's Varieties' – and many other names for the Circus

Alexander Stacey took over the Grand Circus in 1889 and leased it to Dan Leno. The little comedian planned that his mother and stepfather should be in charge and live in a house on the site. They renamed it 'Leno's Varieties' and ran it as a music hall with themselves as top of the bill. The aim was to capitalize on their famous son's huge reputation and, indeed, Leno himself turned up occasionally to dance and sing and to judge the dancing competitions. However, even this venture failed to live up to expectations and it was not long before the Lenos departed. Throughout its relatively short life the building operated under many different names – usually those of current proprietors. So at various times it was advertised as Weldon's Circus, Drake's Circus, Newsome's Circus, Hengler's Circus – but it was always popularly known as the Grand Circus.

The Circus goes up in smoke and the City Theatre rises from the ashes

In 1892, Stacey adopted a new policy and began advertising plays beginning with 'a new and original Irish romantic drama' entitled *Clear-the-Way, or Faugha-Balla.* Then, in May 1893, what would normally have been seen as a disaster turned out to be a blessing in disguise. During the run of *On the Frontier,* a play which featured a spectacular stage fire, the wooden Grand Circus was completely destroyed by a real fire. It was, therefore, relatively easy to clear the site and Stacey immediately set about the construction of a purpose-built theatre right opposite the Royal. 1893 was the year that Sheffield became a city – and on Boxing Day the 'City Theatre' opened with a performance of *A Royal Divorce* by W G Wills and Grace Hawthorn.

Late Victorian music hall patrons had plenty of choice. There were a few larger halls and lots of small ones some of which were so small, and so insignificant, that they were completely unknown outside their immediate neighbourhood. However, as the century drew to a close, everything changed. In 1895, the Empire, a huge music hall with a capacity of 2,500 opened on Charles Street followed a few years later by an even bigger one, the Hippodrome, on Cambridge Street. These two giants effectively put a great many halls out of business. Some survived by becoming cinemas and a few struggled on – but many were forced to close and were lost forever.

Part 3
The Concert Halls

The Music Hall and
The Albert Hall

A letter to the press

MUSIC IN SHEFFIELD

TO THE EDITOR – I have been a visitor in Sheffield for the last six months, and during my stay here have been greatly astonished at the very small amount of interest shown by the inhabitants of this important town regarding high-class concerts and organ recitals. Soon after I came here I went to listen to a very able performer on the magnificent instrument in the Albert Hall. As the prices of admission were decidedly moderate, I was naturally extremely surprised to see row after row of empty seats. On enquiring the reason I was informed by a friend, "Oh, this is nearly always the case with high-class concerts here; don't you know that Sheffielders are not musical?"

I regret to add that my informant's opinion has been clearly confirmed since it was expressed. Let me give a few instances. Take, for example, the two excellent concerts given in October last by the talented members of the various Cathedral choirs on behalf of that worthy charity, the Choir Benevolent Fund. Seat after seat was empty, notwithstanding the good fare provided, and the special object of the concert. Again when those well-known performers, Madame Norman Neruda and Mr. Charles Halle, ventured here, their fears of a scanty audience were fully realised. And when a clever organist gives a recital, the Albert Hall is really (comparatively speaking) empty, as has been shown on several occasions lately, indeed, only last Tuesday, when Mr. W.T. Best, the celebrated organist of St George's Hall, Liverpool, gave two very fine recitals before a miserably small audience. The above are only a few instances which have occurred during the last six months.

Naturally a visitor to this town can only come to the conclusion that the upper classes of society here care little about good music. They are apparently the ones to blame, because at any first rate concert in the Albert Hall it is the commonest occurrence to see 10 or 12 people as the only occupants of one side of the balcony, and I have seen even fewer.

It is really surprising that any townsman can be found with sufficient courage to venture on giving a high class concert, or engaging an expensive organist.

Sheffield, in the way of exhibiting musical interest, is far behind many smaller and less important towns, and is fast running the chance of being looked upon as one of the most unmusical towns in England. Fancy a musical festival taking place in Sheffield and lasting several days! Why the very idea seems ludicrous.

Considering the progress of this great art in the country generally, I cannot understand the apathy of the greater proportion of residents here.
– I am, Sir, your obedient servant,
A LOVER OF "VOCUM ET NERVORUM CANTUS"
31st January, 1883

The Music Hall, Surrey Street

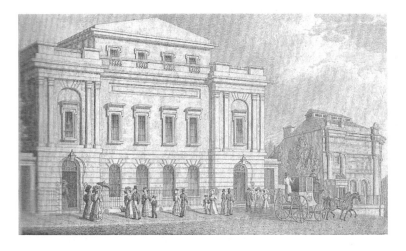

The Music Hall in Surrey Street, which had opened in 1824, was Sheffield's first concert hall. It was a handsome neo-classical building located in the respectable part of town frequented by the professional classes. The proprietors suceeded in cultivating an educated middle-class clientele by offering an attractive range of recitals by international stars such as Angelica Catalani, Paganini and Franz Liszt, as well as high quality choral and orchestral concerts. Smoking was permitted though not encouraged and babes-in-arms were not admitted. The Music Hall provided a tranquil and pleasing alternative to the smoky, noisy lowbrow establishments of West Bar.

Bands, orchestras and instrumentalists

Throughout the Victorian period there were plenty of orchestral and band concerts at the Music Hall. A Viennese Ladies Orchestra went down well (ladies' choirs and orchestras often proved popular especially with gentlemen). There was also a concert by the 'Old Folks' — twenty five men and women from New England all dressed in eighteenth-century period costumes. Popular concerts included Mr Wehli's Orchestral Union which performed on three occasions and regular visits from Charles Hallé and his Manchester 'band'. One of the most notable concerts was provided by thirty three instrumentalists, drawn from Hallé's band and that of Her Majesty's Theatre in a programme of music by a Sheffield celebrity, William Sterndale

Bennett who, at that time, was considered to be one of Europe's outstanding composers. Appearances by military bands ranged from the local Hallamshire Rifles and the Sheffield United Concert Band to the Band of the Coldstream Guards and the Band of the Horse Guards of the King of Hanover who performed 'in full court uniform'.

Musical evenings also featured a wide range of instrumentalists including K P Tommas, the local 'Paganini of the harp,' assisted by his daughters (harp and piano) and the never-to-be-forgotten Herr Sommers and his Sommerophonic Hungarian Musical Company, attired in full native costume, featuring Auguste Dupont, the 'pianiste' and 'from the Grand Ducal Court Theatre, Madlle Therese Manger, Principal Sommerophone Soprano'. There were other rather more sober performances by pianists including Wehli, Clara Linley and, especially, the outstanding Sigismond Thalberg and Emil Bach, a pupil of Franz Liszt. Bach drew a large audience of professional and amateur musicians whose 'rapt attention was a testimony to the performer's display of learning and skill'.[48]

Oratorios and other choral music

Victorian Sheffield had a special affection for choral music. As well as the prestigious Sheffield Choral Society there were several other groups devoted to the promotion of huge choirs. The Sheffield Choral Union, the Sheffield Harmonic Society and the Tonic Sol-fa Choral Society performed all the big oratorios − Haydn's *The Creation* and *The Seasons,* Handel's *Judas Maccabeus* and 'modern' pieces such as Mendelssohn's *St Paul* and *Elijah.* Shorter works − Handel's *Acis and Galatea* and Mendelssohn's *Hymn of Praise* − were also popular. But there is little doubt that Handel's *Messiah* was the favourite. It became obligatory to perform it every Christmas at several venues throughout the town and the Sheffield Choral Society celebrated the centenary of the first performance of this great masterpiece on 28 December 1841.

Not all the choral concerts were of the heavyweight variety. From time to time, evenings were devoted entirely to madrigals. Several visiting choirs regularly put on shows aimed at a rather different market and, as many of these were from foreign parts, they spiced up their performances by appearing in national costume. These included the Ethiopian Serenaders, the Swiss Singers, the Celebrated Hungarian Vocalists and a group of Bernais Singers who came from the French Pyrenees. 'Attired in their National

Costume,' the choir performed their pieces 'without accompaniment, their Voices forming an orchestra.'

Top opera stars in Surrey Street

Recitals by solo singers of international reputation frequently drew large audiences. Many famous opera singers were happy to exchange the stage for the concert platform – and among these were three outstanding sopranos.

The first of these was Jenny Lind, the Swedish Nightingale, by far the biggest star to appear at the Music Hall in the early Victorian period. George Dawson, manager of the Music Hall, finally engaged her to perform on 8 March 1849. For some time there had been a great deal of criticism about the state of the Hall which had recently been described as 'surpassingly dingy, dirty, dismal, disagreeable, discreditable, disreputable and disgraceful'.[*] Dawson hoped that this important performance would encourage the proprietors to refurbish the place but to his disappointment, they approved nothing more than the recovering of the seats in red chintz. Prices reflected the singer's high fee – twenty-one shillings for the main body of the hall (at that time known as the saloon) and ten shillings and sixpence for the gallery. Nevertheless, George Dawson's music shop in Norfolk Street was besieged by crowds of people as soon as tickets went on sale and the road was blocked for several hours. Every seat was sold on the first day but the crowds continued to come and eventually the proprietors agreed to admit eighty people to the orchestra pit at half a guinea each. Again, there were huge queues.

Jennie Lind

---

[*] Letter to the *Independent*, 30. 9.1848.

Jenny Lind duly arrived in Sheffield from Wakefield on the day before her concert. She declined offers of hospitality from 'gentlemen in Sheffield', preferring to stay at the Tontine Hotel near the market. Huge crowds followed her when she went shopping at the cutlery showrooms of Joseph Rodgers and Sons. Long before the evening performance, Surrey Street and Tudor Street were completely blocked by crowds. Like a true celebrity, Jenny took all this in her stride and stood waving and smiling to the crowd for several minutes at the entrance to the theatre.

Unlike the audience of over a thousand who were all in full evening dress, Jenny wore a very simple costume. The reporter from the *Independent* recorded how she moved to the centre of the platform with 'a joyous, bounding gait, stopping to receive the vociferous applause which greeted her from every part of the hall.' He went on to describe her appearance – 'a young woman rather above the average in height and stature and with an expression at once benign, intellectual, hilarious, fascinating'. And then he ran out of adjectives and gave up. 'To attempt description would be futile, to criticize impossible. We are met by a sense of the utter absurdity of attempting to describe in print the most wonderful, the most brilliant and the most varied of vocal powers it has ever been our lot to witness. One might as well attempt to put into words the warbling of the thrush or of the nightingale.' [49]

After several encores, Jenny joined in the singing of the national anthem which was taken up by the crowds waiting outside to escort her carriage back to the Tontine Hotel. Accustomed as she was to distinguished and enthusiastic audiences, she must have been particularly touched by her Sheffield supporters for she sent the people of the town a message that 'the heartiness of her Sheffield audience was peculiarly to her taste'. Jenny Lind was a generous woman and wherever she appeared she gave a percentage of her fee to local charities.

If anything, the demand for tickets was even greater when she returned on 31 March, 1856. The enthusiasm of the audience was such that the concert did not finish until after eleven o'clock and the crowds did not disperse until after midnight. This time, however, the local press was much less enthusiastic and the *Independent* gave it a lukewarm review saying that 'the truth must be told, the peerless Jenny was *husky*!' [50]

With her husband, Otto Goldschmidt, as her accompanist, Jenny's third and final visit to the Music Hall took place on 27 March 1862. Tickets were again highly priced at one guinea, half-a-guinea and seven shillings and again they were a sell-out. There appear to have been traces of fatigue in the famous voice but 'all the old characteristic graces of style, the endless pearly roulades, the delicate trills and the marvellous scales were as noteworthy as in her earlier days'.[51]

Jenny was not the only superstar songstress in Victorian times. 'There is only one Niagara,' she wrote with admiration, 'and there is only one Patti.' She felt that Adelina Patti's lucrative career had equalled if not surpassed her own. Indeed Patti, who began performing professionally at the age of ten, was billed as 'La Petite Jenny Lind.' By the time she came to Sheffield in 1861 she was one of the principal stars at Covent Garden and tickets were quickly sold out. Despite her reputation, prices were low compared with those for Jenny Lind, only five shillings for a reserved orchestra stall and three shillings for a reserved seat in the Music Hall's small gallery. [52]   An eager and expectant audience greeted an attractive young woman described as having a 'sweet, expressive and characterful face, not much above five feet tall and with a trim figure'. The concert was a huge success and delighted both the public and the press − yet it was nearly thirty years before Patti returned to perform at the Albert Hall in November 1889.

Adelina Patti

Giulia Grisi

Giulia Grisi, Queen Victoria's favourite singer, was another opera star to appear at the Music Hall. She was not only extremely beautiful but also an astute business woman. She was accompanied by the handsome Giovanni Mario, her partner and companion for more than thirty years, who took part in the performances. Her first concert in 1845 was arranged by the Sheffield Athenaeum whose members were allocated seats by lottery. Although the hall was full, she was not offered the rapturous reception enjoyed by Lind and Patti but she visited again during her farewell tour in 1861.

95

Lind, Patti and Grisi – the world's greatest sopranos all appeared in Sheffield in the space of six months!

Other highly regarded (and highly paid) stars found their way to the Surrey Street concert hall. A few months after Jenny Lind made her final appearance, the Athenaeum put on a concert with, according to the *Independent,* 'one of the finest casts ever introduced to our audience.' Topping the bill were the tenor, Antonio Giuglini, and the soprano, Thérèse Tietiens* – two of the biggest stars of the day. The *Independent* was particularly impressed by the singing of Tietiens:

> Of her execution we cannot speak too highly in most respects. Singularly distinct and bell-like in the slower passages, the scales are so smooth as almost to suggest the idea of a slide and the ear is not only charmed but deceived. On the whole we must say we have rarely heard any singing which will bear comparison with that of Mdlle Tietiens; her dramatic power is, if possible, even greater than her vocal. Her reception was most enthusiastic.[53]

When Jenny Lind gave her final concert at the Music Hall she was supported by Signor Belletti and the English tenor and opera star Sims Reeves, a favourite singer who was a regular visitor to Sheffield throughout the second half of the nineteenth century. Other top musicians and singers sometimes found the Sheffield public apathetic but Sims Reeves always seemed able to get decent audiences for his concerts. People were more than willing to turn out to hear England's most famous tenor.

Charles Hallé brings his Orchestra

Charles Hallé was another regular visitor in the late Victorian period. Time after time, from the 1860s onwards, he made trips across the Pennines to perform as a solo pianist, play duets with the virtuoso violinist Wilma Norman-Neruda (his future wife) and, especially in later years, to conduct his full orchestra of eighty players. We can only be amazed at his patience and persistence for more often than not his concerts at the Music Hall and the Albert Hall played to poor houses. In 1869 the *Independent* noted that the audience was 'not so numerous as must be deserved' adding rather

---

* Her name was also spelt 'Tietjens' All references to her in the Sheffield press are spelt 'Tietiens'.

lamely 'there have been numerous concerts this season'.[54] Another concert found the local press acutely embarrassed:

> We have so often had to complain of the niggardly support accorded to Mr Hallé in his Sheffield ventures, that we almost feel ashamed to chronicle the conspicuousness of long rows of empty seats. It is out of the question to suggest that performances such as that of last night can be expected to appeal to the general public or even to the considerable class that believes it loves good music; but in Sheffield there are surely sufficient amateurs, professing taste and intelligence, to fill the Surrey Street room, and to speak plainly, it is a direct reproach to them that such gifted artistes as Mr Hallé and Madame Norman-Neruda have, time after time, to be content with the demonstrations of the ardent few instead of the acclamations of a good "house."[55]

Wilma Norman-Neruda and Charles Hallé

In an otherwise excellent review the reporter did mention that Hallé's performance was less obviously expressive than that of Norman-Neruda whose more flamboyant style offered 'a striking contrast now and then to the remarkably learned and unobtrusive method of her coadjutor.'[*]

Hallé continued to make regular visits to the Music Hall, and later the Albert Hall. Finally, in the late eighties, Sheffield began to show some interest in serious music and Hallé and his new wife began to get the appreciation that they thoroughly deserved.

---

[*] Although Hallé was a fine technician who immersed himself in his music, his performances were generally rather low-key.

Amateur Dramatics: Charles Dickens and friends

From its earliest days the Music Hall, like most concert halls, needed to do more than provide a platform for classical music – in fact it offered a wide variety of entertainment although in general it was careful not to upset the sensibilities of its rather puritanical clientele. One of the most exciting events at the Music Hall involved Charles Dickens.

Dickens was not only a brilliant novelist – he was also an outstanding amateur actor. For some time he and a group of friends had been putting on plays for their own amusement and it occurred to Dickens that this could be a way to raise money for one of his pet schemes, the Guild of Literature and Art. They got off to a flying start with a performance at the Duke of Devonshire's London residence before a select gathering which included Queen Victoria and Prince Albert.

Other engagements quickly followed and on Monday 30 August, 1852 Dickens and his company were booked to appear at the Music Hall. This created quite a stir and excitement in the town ran high. Every seat was sold as soon as booking opened.

The visit was not without difficulties for the company not only brought scenery, properties, costumes and curtains – they brought their own stage as well. The architect, Sir Joseph Paxton, had designed the stage for the London performance and the company insisted on performing on it. The problem was to fit this stage into the Music Hall without seriously reducing its capacity. It was finally decided to board over the existing dais and orchestra pit and fit Paxton's stage on top.

An army of carpenters arrived in advance to transform the Music Hall into a full-blown theatre. Silk souvenir programmes were on sale to a glittering audience of Sheffield's elite in full evening dress. A new three-act comedy by Sir Edward Bulwer-Lytton, *Not So Bad As We Seem or Many Sides to a Character,* was the main offering of the evening. The local critic, damning with faint praise, declared that the play had many fine touches of sentiment and not a few touches of humour but it was somewhat deficient in character and plot. 'There is not a single scene that palls upon the senses, but there is not a situation that commands wondering admiration'. But Charles Dickens shone as Lord Wilmot, and as Curll the bookseller and displayed 'the most extraordinary talent.' The cast included a number of eminent Victorians including the novelist Wilkie

Collins, Mark Lemon the editor of *Punch*, the artist Augustus Egg and John Tenniel the illustrator of *Alice in Wonderland*.

The long evening ended with a one-act farce, *Mr Nightingale's Diary,* specially written by Mark Lemon and Dickens himself − and they made sure that it was a showcase for their considerable acting talents. The plot demanded that Lemon and Dickens dressed up as various characters. Lemon played three parts and Dickens who began as a lawyer, Mr Grabblewick, also reappeared at various times as Charley Bit (a boots), Mr Poulter, Captain Blower, a respectable female and a deaf sexton.[*]

John Tenniel   Mark Lemon

Augustus Egg   Charles Dickens

[*] See *Plays and Poems of Charles Dickens,* Vol.II, London 1885. The original playbill for this performance can be seen on the walls of the Lyceum Theatre.

This little piece was a huge success and the *Independent* was bowled over by Dickens' performance. 'There is ample opportunity for the development of fun and eccentricity. The genius of Mr Dickens is truly versatile. Is it possible that on the stage he could as effectually move the deeper and more sacred feelings of our nature? If he can do so – as he can with his pen picture such beings as Little Nell, Paul Dombey and Agnes – then might he be one of the greatest actors that ever lived.'[56]

At the end of the evening the entire cast took curtain calls, still a rare event in the nineteenth century. Dickens and his party stayed the night at the Royal Hotel and later expressed themselves well pleased with their reception in Sheffield. The evening raised £190 for the Guild.

Lectures and readings

The Music Hall also offered special lecture evenings featuring celebrated personalities including the novelist, William Makepeace Thackeray and Henry Bishop, one of the leading musicians of the day.[*] But the biggest celebrities by far were Lola Montez, P T Barnum, Fanny Kemble and, once again, Charles Dickens who delighted audiences with readings from his novels[**]. He came to Sheffield on four occasions, making his final visit in 1869, just before he retired, including the ever popular *A Christmas Carol* in his programme.

Lola Montez

In February 1859, Lola Montez, Countess of Landsfeld – Spanish dancer, actress and adventuress – drew a full house to hear a talk on 'Comic Aspects of Fashion'. Sheffield was delighted to welcome such a sensationally interesting character whose many adventures had received much attention in the Press. It promised to be a most exciting evening. The *Independent* devoted a good deal of space to the event and an amused reporter noted that

[*] Henry Bishop, conductor and composer, was the first musician to receive a knighthood and was famous for his composition 'Home Sweet Home', one of the best-known ballads of the nineteenth century.
[**] Dickens did the first of these readings on 22 December 1855 at the Mechanics' Institute on the corner of Surrey Street and Tudor Street.

100

most of the tickets had been sold to gentlemen. In the event it proved to be rather a damp squib. Lola's costume was far from exotic. She wore a tasteful black velvet high-necked dress with a little lace collar and lace undersleeves. Her face bore the 'impress of remarkable beauty' but had 'suffered from the ravages of time'. Although she looked a little wan and haggard, she spoke distinctly and could be clearly heard throughout the house. The lecture was also 'in good taste', something of a disappointment to those 'gentlemen' who had been hoping for something rather less tasteful and rather more tasty. Lola left the platform without waiting for either questions or applause but the audience was insistent and she eventually made a reluctant reappearance and took a bow.[57]

Perhaps the biggest show-business personality of the nineteenth century was the American, Phineas Taylor Barnum. Famous for the catch phrase 'there's a sucker born every minute', Barnum described himself as the Prince of 'Humbug' – that special quality by which he aimed to persuade the 'suckers' to part with their money. Unlike the full house drawn by the lovely Lola, Barnum only managed to attract a very small audience. He announced that he would speak on the science of money-making and his definition of 'Humbug', supporting his theory with 'pictorial illustrations and original anecdotes, examples and experience'. Sheffield was not impressed:

P T Barnum

The former part of Mr. Barnum's address was common-place and somewhat tedious. The latter portion, however, which was devoted to the exposition of 'humbug', was amusing from the utterly outrageous character of the stories and statements it comprised, and was not only exposition but a veritable illustration of the particular commodity with which Barnum has become synonymous. The number humbugged, however, to the credit of the town be it said, was far from large, the Music Hall not being more than one quarter filled. Mr. Barnum delivers his address with great freedom and self-possession, but does not appear to merit the very high encomiums which have been bestowed upon his elocution etc. by some of the London papers.[58]

After the lecture the audience was given a chance to see Barnum's 'renowned' mermaid.

In 1850, Fanny Kemble accompanied by her daughter, offered an impressive evening of Shakespeare. She delivered from memory the whole of the three act edition of *The Taming of the Shrew* and her daughter recited the Balcony Scene from *Romeo and Juliet* and the Closet Scene from *Hamlet*. Fanny, whose theatrical family had strong connections with Sheffield, was extremely popular and her three visits in 1850, 1851 and 1852 were all over-subscribed.[*]

Other entertainment at the Music Hall

The Music Hall was rarely continuously booked so engagements could be arranged at short notice and artists who proved popular could extend their run until the public tired of them. There was plenty to choose from.

Panoramas could always be relied on to bring in large audiences and there was great excitement when, in December 1845, a 'Novel Exhibition of Aeronautikon or Grand Vertical and Horizontal Moving Panorama' was announced. The 'Aeronautikon' was certainly something special. As great reels of painted canvas slowly unrolled to appropriate music, spectators were invited to enter the car of the balloon in London's Vauxhall Gardens and were gently wafted over the City and along the Thames to Greenwich. Then on they went to Dover, the Channel, Calais by moonlight and finally to the Rhine Valley. They were also treated to aerial views of places visited by Queen Victoria on her tour of Germany, twenty 'Colossal Views' of Hong Kong and several views of Sir Charles Napier's Conquests of India. There

---

[*] In their day, the Kembles were probably England's most important theatrical family. Fanny's aunt, Sarah Siddons, and uncle, John Philip Kemble, were leading actors and another uncle, Stephen, was manager of the Theatre in Sheffield for a time. Her father, Charles, made his first stage appearance in the town at the age of seventeen. See *Georgian Theatre in Sheffield* for details of the Kemble family's relationship with Sheffield.

102

was a 'diorama of the Shrine of the Holy Nativity at Bethlehem, both by day and by night', and the whole show was accompanied by a descriptive lecture. After all this, the management threw in a couple of Scottish dancers and the 'elegant and admired Negro melodists' to round off the performance. There were two shows every day at normal prices – two shillings, one shilling or sixpence in the gallery and children at half price. Many thousands flocked to see the show and they certainly got their money's worth.[59]

Minstrel shows were another big attraction. They had become popular in America in the 1840s and within a decade had crossed the Atlantic and taken London by storm. Their fame soon spread to the provinces and, in November 1859, one of the most famous troupes, the Christy Minstrels, paid its first visit to Sheffield to the delight of the press and the public. From then on they were frequent visitors entertaining huge audiences with their black-faced song and dance routines. They had many imitators. Other troupes included the 'Georgia Minstrels' and a somewhat strange group called 'The Female Christys' who represented Amazons and were inexplicably clad in silver armour. It all sounds rather wonderful!

TO-NIGHT

MUSIC HALL   SURREY STREET

FOR TWO NIGHTS ONLY.

TUESDAY AND WEDNESDAY
Nov. 30th AND Dec .1st

FAREWELL TOUR OF THE WORLD-RENOWNED

FEMALE CHRISTYS

Fifteen Unrivalled LADY ARTISTES dressed in real silver Armour,
representing the Amazons of the Silver City of Atlantis in their New and
Superb Programme, challenging the world for Originality, Dash and Brilliancy
A GRAND, GORGEOUS, GLORIOUS, GLITTERING,
GIGANTIC and UNIQUE ENTERTAINMENT
The only Organized Female Troupe in the World Admission   2s., 1s., and
6d.
Doors open at Half-past Seven; Commence at Eight
Carriages at Ten o'clock
Sole Proprietor............Mr. ANDY MERRILEES

Victorians also loved ghost stories. Dozens of plays and short stories, designed to make the hair stand on end, were written about supernatural events. The Spectral Opera Company with the famous 'Pepper's Ghost' illusion provided the Christmas show in 1876. It played to twenty thousand people over a five week run then moved to the rival Albert Hall in Barker's Pool for another two weeks. The Company performed *Faust,* and two plays, *A Christmas Carol* and *The Haunted House.*[*]

The latter was described as one of the most extraordinary entertainments:

> Ordinary ghost illusions sink into utter insignificance in comparison with what Mr Fred Smith, the proprietor, is able to accomplish. In *The Haunted House,* which is justly described as a spectral farce, spectres suddenly appear and as suddenly disappear. They apparently make their way through deal boards, they come on from the wings, they push their heads through boxes, they climb up the back of the stage and revolve in defiance of all known laws. Finally, after frightening the unfortunate inhabitant of the haunted house nearly out of his wits, they make him one of themselves and he appears and disappears with as much ease as they, and with as much apparent enjoyment.[60]

The show was so terrifying that there were shrieks from the audience and some people, unable to stand the excitement, had to leave the hall.

Variety acts came in all shapes and sizes and included a couple of well-known wizards. 'Professor' John Henry Anderson, the 'Great Wizard of the North' was one of those performers who invariably managed to extend his engagements. Anderson first came to the Music Hall in 1838 and was a frequent visitor for the next twenty five years. He was a great self-publicist and whenever he visited Sheffield he flooded the town with handbills, posters and press notices – and it always paid off. He certainly did not do things by halves. When je brought his daughters to the Music Hall Miss Anderson was billed as 'the Modern Mnemosyne and Retro-reminiscent Orthographist', Miss E Anderson, 'the Ariel to Prospero', and Miss Flora Anderson, 'the Fairy of the Mystic Scene'. The show ran for several weeks.

---

[*] Pepper's Ghost, using light and a system of mirrors, was able to create spectacular effects which enabled the audience to see through solid objects.

GUN TRICK ! ! !

Of which he is the SOLE INVENTOR

Mr. J. H. A. will allow any gentleman to charge a Fowling Piece with Powder and Bullets, in the presence of the whole audience, previously marking the Balls so as to ascertain them again. He will be desired to fire at Mr. A. who will receive the Balls in his hands, on his Face, or any part of his Body the Audience may direct, being upwards of the thousandth time of his attempting this experiment.

  Any gentleman will be allowed to bring his own Fowling Piece and Ingredients for Loading.

J H Anderson, the Wizard of the North

Another popular visitor was Jacobs, the Wizard of Wizards, who styled himself a 'modern magician, ventriloquist, Professor of Experimental Philosophy and improvisator'. He too enjoyed an extended run but he was no match for the 'Wizard of the North'.

Mr and Mrs Howard Paul who made regular visits to the Music Hall were one of its greatest attractions. Their shows containing a mixture of songs, impersonations, and parodies (very often of opera) seem to have had just the right ingredients for those for whom the real thing was rather too heavy and indigestible. An advertisement for a show in February 1861 includes Mr Howard Paul singing a 'new buffo scene descriptive of the calamities that befell The Damp Troubadour' and Mrs Howard Paul provided a 'marvellous living photograph (in costume) of Mr Sims Reeves as Robin Hood.' The Sims Reeves impersonation was subsequently included in just about every show the couple gave in Sheffield – reflecting both the quality of Mrs Howard Paul's performance and Mr Reeve's popularity in the town.

Mr and Mrs Howard Paul

There were many performers at the Music Hall who would have been quite at home down in West Bar. Tom Thumb was the stage name frequently adopted by a number of celebrated dwarfs, but the most famous of these was the American, Charles Sherwood Stratton who, thanks to Barnum, became a world-wide celebrity as 'General' Tom Thumb. When he came to Sheffield in 1857 at the age of nineteen, he had reached his full height of three feet four inches. Audiences flocked to the Music Hall to see him portray various historical characters including

Tom Thumb

106

Ghosts

Victorians loved ghost stories and it is no surprise that ghostly characters very often turned up on stage. In 1862, Professor John Henry Pepper gave a demonstration showing how, using lighting and a glass screen, wonderful effects could be created. Characters could disappear and reappear and a room and its contents could change before the eyes of the audience. It was not long before these ghostly effects found their way to Sheffield. In 1863, Tommy Youdan's first season in his newly upgraded Surrey Theatre included a drama called *Faith, Hope and Charity* which featured 'Pepper's Ghost'.

In the same year more ghostly goings on were to be found at the Theatre Royal. Charles Pitt obtained exclusive rights to use a patented system devised by H N King. Although, we are not exactly sure how King's ghost effect worked, there is no doubt it was extremely effective. *The Dead Witness,* specially written by Wybert Reeve to show off the ghost effects, delighted the man from the *Independent.* It was, he said, 'one of the most extraordinary stage effects ever produced. The ghost appears and disappears. An attempt to run it through with a sword pierces only air. Later the spirit comes forth apparently through walls with all the apparent substance and reality of flesh and blood, hands over a note to prove the villain's guilt and then, when approached, becomes a shadow. The effect is marvellous'. Pitt realized that he was on to a good thing and used King's system in four other plays – an adaptation of Dickens' *A Christmas Carol, Raymond and Agnes* with its spectre of the bleeding nun, *The Phantom's Bride*, and Monk Lewis's gothic horror story, *The Castle Spectre.*

Those who flocked to see Henry Irving in *The Bells* when he brought his Lyceum Company to Sheffield clearly enjoyed his much praised performance as Matthias but also must have been thrilled by the scenic effects. This time the magic was provided by theatrical gauzes which, skilfully lit, enabled Mathias (and the audience) to see, through a seemingly solid wall, a vision of the Jew he had killed fifteen years earlier. In Act 3, Mathias's bedroom wall melts away to reveal an entire courtroom, the scene of a nightmare in which he is forced to confess his guilt. Effects like these must have contributed to the phenomenal success of the play.

The Spectral Opera Company, dedicated to providing thrilling, supernatural entertainment, visited both Sheffield concert halls in the 1870s and showed that Professor Pepper's effects had lost none of their power to terrify the audience. A performance of *The Haunted House* at the Music Hall was so realistic that people cried out and sometimes had to leave the hall. This show provided a treat for the children of Sheffield Workhouse and the boys of Sheffield Charity School. Not only were the youngsters scared out of their wits – the management gave them all an orange in addition to letting them in for nothing. It must have been a wonderful evening out!

Napoleon and Frederick the Great as well as 'a Highlander, an Oxonian, a sailor, and a variety of statues from classical antiquity'. Always impeccably dressed in appropriate costume, he danced and sang a number of popular songs of the day such as 'Bobbing Around', 'My Mary Ann' and 'Villikins and his Dinah.'

Frederic Maccabe, another very versatile performer, first appeared at the Music Hall in 1866 and returned many times with his one-man show

Frederic Maccabe

Begone Dull Care. Maccabe, a musician, composer, mimic, ventriloquist and well known 'portrayer of character', changed his programme daily and the hall was crowded for every performance. 'The great hit last night' said the *Independent*, 'was the burlesque of Sir Rowland the Ruff-un in which Mr Maccabe appears as a complete theatrical company, and supplies a first class melodrama, highly spiced with sensational effects, by his own unaided efforts.'[61] He provided a delightful send-up of the kind of thing which could regularly be found round the corner at the Theatre Royal.

The local press, reflecting the strong puritan elements among its readers, welcomed performers who provided good, wholesome entertainment. One of their favourites was Arthur Lloyd, a music hall singer, who arranged popular concerts which included a comic element. When he first came to Sheffield in 1866, he brought with him a number of acts from London's Oxford and Canterbury music halls, such as the tenor, Frank Raynor, and the ventriloquist, W B Alexander. The *Independent* commented that 'All Mr Lloyd's songs, which are free from coarseness, were most rapturously received.'[62]

Arthur Lloyd – 'free from coarsness'

And they liked Harry Liston, a North country comedian, who made his name in London but never forgot his origins. He frequently visited the Music Hall with his solo show *Merry Moments.*

His entertainment may well be called *Merry Moments* for his audiences scarcely ever cease to laugh...... He has been aptly called the 'Prince of Singing Comedians' as he fully justifies that title...... With such versatility it cannot be a matter of wonder that Mr Liston's entertainments are so popular especially when they are free from the least taint of vulgarity. Last night he appeared in a round of his most popular characters, both male and female, and was loudly applauded on every appearance.'[63]

Mr Lloyd's songs, 'free from coarseness,' and Mr Liston's act, 'free from the least taint of vulgarity,' were just the thing for the Music Hall's respectable middle-class audiences.

However, performances by Alfred Peek Stevens, the Great Vance, were less well received by the local press. He was a friend and rival of George Leybourne, 'Champagne Charlie,' and their flamboyant lifestyle hardly endeared them to some of the more straight-laced Victorians. *The Independent* did not think much of Stevens' first visit in 1867:

> The name of "the great Vance" was sufficient to attract a numerous and very respectable audience, a large number of whom were ladies, and this fact should have induced Mr Vance to be very careful in his selection. Instead, however, of this being the case, his songs, whatever may be thought of them in London music halls, were, we venture to think, anything but suitable to the audience who assembled in our music hall last evening; and one of his selections especially was of such a questionable character that, to say the least, it would have been much better omitted.[64]

But Vance returned to the Music Hall the following year and again in 1872. Perhaps the ladies actually enjoyed their evening out and came back for more of the same.

In 1876, the management of the Music Hall booked a celebrity named Morgan – who happened to be a dog! Morgan had become a star when he discovered the body of Emily Holland, victim of a notorious Blackburn murderer. Thomas Parkinson, his owner, capitalized on his pet's fame by exhibiting him at fairs, shows and halls all over the country. Other canny dog owners quickly cashed in on his idea by rechristening their own dogs and when Thomas Parkinson arrived in Sheffield he was dismayed to find that another Morgan was advertised to appear at the Royal Alhambra Music Hall in Union Street. An affronted Mr Parkinson was obliged to put a notice in a local paper denouncing the imposter. [65]

A concert hall in decline – the final humiliation

By the 1870s, The Music Hall was struggling and, although there were some concerts, it was increasingly reliant on other events to make ends meet. Towards the end of the decade, competition from the newer, modern Albert Hall in Barker's Pool was having an adverse effect and the hall, now over fifty years old, was in serious trouble. The proprietors were relieved to find an alternative source of income when the Sheffield High School for Girls used it as a temporary home from 1878 to 1884, while its purpose-built premises in Rutland Park were under construction. When the school moved out, they seriously considered selling but in the end they restored the organ and, after some modest redecoration, reopened the building for public performances. A few artists, including Charles Hallé, continued to perform there but most of the regulars now preferred the Albert Hall.[*] The proprietors did little to halt the gradual slide into dilapidation and in the end the Music Hall became the venue mainly for amateur performances of Handel's *Messiah* and similar popular works but even these were few and far between.

After a further lick of paint the proprietors' booking agent advertised that it was available for concerts, meetings, balls and bazaars, but there were hardly any takers and in 1892 the United Gas Light Company hired the hall to exhibit its wares. This was the final humiliation. What had once been described as 'a spacious and elegant building in the Grecian style,'[**] a building graced by Paganini, Catalani, Liszt, Jenny Lind and Charles Dickens, was now no more than a sooty old building full of gas stoves.

---

[*] Because of its design the acoustics at the Music Hall were excellent and Hallé and his wife Norman-Neruda always enjoyed performing there.

[**] Samuel Lewis, *A Topographical Dictionary of England,* 1835. See also *Georgian Theatre in Sheffield,* p 77.

The Albert Hall, Barker's Pool

By the late 1850s, demand was increasing for a bigger and better concert hall to cater for the growing taste for cultural events, particularly musical entertainment. The dilapidated Music Hall in Surrey Street was unsuitable for conversion and Thomas Youdan's ideas for redesigning his unused Adelphi theatre as a 4,000-seater concert hall had come to nothing. On 17 May 1861, a group of local businessmen met to discuss ideas to set up a project ' to provide, in a central position in the town of Sheffield, in the County of York, a hall for musical and other purposes, capable of seating comfortably 3,000 persons'.[*] The Sheffield Music Hall Company Ltd was formed.

Slow progress on the new concert hall

The new Company immediately set about raising the fairly modest sum of £15,000 for construction of the hall through the sale of 500 shares of £30. It was estimated that £8,000 would be needed for the building itself, £3,000 for an organ and furnishings and the rest for the purchase of a suitable site.   Plans were drawn up to build and equip the hall by Christmas 1868 but after a

---

[*] Details of the meeting were later recorded in the *Independent* 2.2. 1869.

promising start, enthusiasm began to wane and by the end of 1867 only three-fifths of the capital had been raised. It was nine long years before the foundation stone was laid by the Duke of Norfolk on 1 September, 1870. A site had been purchased on the corner of Barker's Pool and the event drew an enormous crowd. The Duke was accompanied by local dignitaries who spoke at some length.

First came the President of the Music Hall Company, Sir John Brown, who pointed out that when the existing Music Hall was planned in 1822, the population of the town was 65,000 – it was now well over 200,000 and it was clear that what was right for Sheffield in the 1820s was no longer satisfactory. He said he had endeavoured to do what he could to produce music and entertainments of a character which would not demoralize, but would instruct and edify and cultivate the taste for amusements of a refining tendency, and he set the building which they commenced that day against the numberless buildings in Sheffield today of a very opposite character, and having exactly the reverse tendency.

The Mayor of Sheffield, Alderman Thomas Moore, then made a direct appeal for more money. Sheffield had needed a new concert hall for some time and he called on the town's *nouveaux riches* to lend greater financial support to the project. He did not see why they should make so much money and not refine their tastes. It was no good to have merely amassed money unless they could amass intelligence and good taste with it. He should be very glad indeed if they could have a few more gentlemen coming forward to assist them to complete their work. He could not promise very large dividends. He supposed that was one reason why they had not come forward. If he could promise them 10, 15, or 20 per cent no doubt that he could get rid of a hundred thousand shares that day. But where the idea was to refine taste and cultivate intelligence they were often backward.

The Choral Union, who had opened the proceedings with 'Hail, Smiling Morn' then celebrated the laying of the stone with the Hallelujah Chorus. Finally, the Master Cutler, William Bragge praised this exciting new project but at the same time expressed the hope that it would inspire greater efforts to provide much needed improvements in the living conditions of the poorer communities in Sheffield. The first nobleman in England had come to lay the foundation stone for the working men of one of the dirtiest cities of Europe. They wanted in Sheffield music halls, but they wanted also something as a preparation for music halls. They wanted washing places which he hoped would come in due time. He would not

113

say that they were beginning at the wrong end by building edifices for pleasure. Certainly not. But he hoped that edifices for pleasure would bring in their turn edifices for cleanliness, and edifices for the education of the lowest classes and for things which were really and truly necessary.[66]

The stone had been laid, the speeches were over, the hallelujahs died away, the huge crowd dispersed – and everything went on just as slowly as before.

Completion at last – a disappointing building but a wonderful organ

By the time the initial funding target was reached in 1872, the estimated cost had risen by £5,000 and there was a further issue of £30 shares. The main structure of the building was eventually completed in March 1873 and arrangements were made for the construction of a large concert organ.

Overall there was not much to recommend the appearance of the hall. It was of 'red brick relieved by granite pillars and a carved stone cornice and tracings, remarkable rather for hugeness of appearance than for external beauty'.[*] And it did not improve with age. Twenty years later, it was described as 'an extraordinary vulgar mass, with heavy Gothic foliage ornament, and a classical cornice'.[**] Inside, there was a main hall, 125 feet long by 60 feet wide encircled by a promenade. To save money, the height had been reduced to a mere 50 feet, much lower than originally planned. There was a balcony along three sides with a narrow gallery and ten arcades above. There was also a smaller hall measuring 60 feet by 40 feet. That the hall was far from beautiful was almost certainly not the fault of the architects, Messrs Flockton and Abbot. Lack of funds had dictated economies and sadly the Albert Hall never aspired to become a centre of musical excellence on a par with Birmingham, Liverpool, Manchester and Leeds.

Fortunately, however, the superb concert organ did much to compensate for the architectural shortcomings for it was built by Aristide Cavaillé-Coll, the best organ builder in Europe. The Rev Sir Frederick A Gore Ouseley, Bart., Professor of Music at Oxford, was invited to test the installation and pronounced that 'the organ would be a very magnificent instrument

---

[*] *The Illustrated Guide to Sheffield 1879.*
[**] *The Builder,* 9 October 1897.

when completed.' By December 1873, Sheffield found itself the possessor of the finest organ in the country.

> Whatever may be said in praise or blame of the architectural character and external appearance of the new Music Hall, in Barker Pool there cannot be two opinions respecting the magnificent organ erected in the large hall by M. Cavaillé-Coll, of Paris. It is not often that we in Sheffield can pride ourselves of being ahead of other large towns in public spirit; more often we are in the background, treading our way "with slow and measured steps," whilst towns of less population and much less importance are taking prominent positions in the van. It becomes a real pleasure to be able to say that for once Sheffield has gone far ahead of all other towns and that in a direction which might hardly have been expected.[67]

The instrument was enormous. It contained 5,000 pipes, 76 stops and four consoles, perfect for providing an accompaniment for choral concerts which were becoming increasingly popular in the town. At first, its massive size was something of a drawback for the instrument needed several men to blow it and the noise could clearly be heard in the auditorium. After several attempts the problem was eventually solved by the introduction of a small gas engine.[*]

Aristide Cavaillé-Coll

The new hall opens

The hall finally opened on Monday 15th December 1873 with a morning organ recital by W T Best, 'organist of London's Albert Hall and the St George's Hall, Liverpool', and an evening performance of *Messiah* under the direction of R S Burton of Leeds. With the opening came a new name. So far it had been known as the 'New Music Hall' but the proprietors of the old Music Hall strongly objected to this and, like so many other buildings all over the country, it was rechristened the Albert Hall, in

---

[*] See *Sheffield Red Book* for 1883. Some twenty years later there was concern about a second problem for this splendid instrument was not tuned to what had become the 'concert pitch' adopted by several major orchestras and extensive (and expensive) re-tuning had to be carried out.

memory of the late Prince Consort.

Every effort was made to do justice to the magnificent organ and indeed it attracted some of the finest musicians of the day. These included Charles-Marie Widor, one of the most influential of all nineteenth-century European organists. He gave three concerts but in spite of very low ticket prices audiences were 'wretchedly small'. Félix-Alexandre Guilmant another outstanding Parisian organist also found the audiences very small and 'generally unappreciative'.

Charles-Marie Vidor   *Félix -Alexandre Guilmant*

Although his visits to the Music Hall in Surrey Street had drawn only poor audiences Charles Hallé had never given up on Sheffield. Early in January 1874, he brought his full company of sixty-five first-class performers to the Albert Hall. As well as the violinist Madame Wilma Norman-Neruda who together with Herr Strauss performed Bach's double violin concerto, there was a vocalist, Madame Lemens Sherrington, and Hallé himself played piano solos. Hallé had done everything he could to help the new hall on its way yet classical concerts and recitals was generally disappointing and the *Independent* was despondent: 'A great deal yet remains to be done in the matter of educating the masses of the people of Sheffield to a right appreciation of really good music'.[68]

There were a few exceptions. John Sims Reeves, Sheffield's favourite tenor and a stalwart of the Music Hall, gave his first concert at the Albert Hall in August 1874 and returned several times. He had lost none of his popular appeal − but then his 'ballad concerts' were perhaps rather less demanding than those of the classical organists and orchestras.

Minstrel Shows

One of the most popular forms of entertainment in Sheffield was the Minstrel Show. All over the town groups of men would put on black faces and curly wigs and perform standard routines to delighted audiences.

The rise of the Minstrel shows was extremely rapid. A group calling themselves 'The Virginia Minstrels' first performed in New York in 1843. Within a year another blackface troupe played before the President at the White House. Many more followed including the Christy Minstrels who played on Broadway for ten years and set the standard for a typical performance with dancers and musicians, the comic 'end men' and the white-faced 'interlocutor.' Stephen Foster wrote 'The Camptown Races' and several other popular songs for the Christy troupe.

Minstrel shows crossed the Atlantic and soon became popular in both London and the provinces — and, in 1859, the original Christy Minstrels came to the Music Hall in Surrey Street. From then on a variety of troupes were regular performers at both the Music Hall and the Albert Hall. A number of them either pretended to be the original Christys or included the name in their title. 'Christys', 'Tute's Great Christy Minstrels' and 'Female Christys' (bizarrely clad in silver armour) all performed in Sheffield along with a great many others including 'Matthew's Minstrels', Sam Hague's 'Original Slave Troupe' and the 'Caledonian Minstrels'.

Performances were by no means confined to the two concert halls, There were minstrel shows at the Grand Circus in the town centre, Dwight's Maryland Minstrels turned up at Youdan's Surrey Music Hall in West Bar and similar shows such as The Montague Christy Minstrels and the Royal Marionette Minstrels could even be found at 'respectable' venues like the Temperance Hall in Townhead Street. The Temperance Hall also welcomed Professor Balme, a 'mesmerist' who added an interesting twist to his performance. At the end of his act, a number of people who had been 'mesmerized' were 'made to go through the performance of a band of christy minstrels, with the usual songs, laughable sayings and conundrums'.

It seems that just about everyone in Sheffield loved a Minstrel Show.

Lowbrow acts at the Albert Hall

The apathetic response of the people of Sheffield to the new hall was a great blow. Income was poor and the proprietors were seriously worried. And so, like their predecessors at the Music Hall, they were driven to engaging other kinds of entertainers. One such was Mr Pemberton Willard. 'Not content with appearing in the costumes of many countries, he plays what might not inaptly be described as the national instrument, oftentimes with very considerable effect'.[69] The strategy worked. When it was realized that the Albert Hall was not exclusively a classical music venue, audiences began to grow and some artists who had been regulars in Surrey Street now began to appear in Barker's Pool. These included the Hamiltons' immensely popular Dioramas which provided a reliable source of income:

> The house was last evening well filled with a most enthusiastic audience which was not slow in testifying their pleasure. The paintings, which are of a most superior description, are all taken either from sketches by Mr Hamilton or from photographs, and represent many places of interest on the overland route (to India). Some novel mechanical effects were introduced, which increased the enthusiasm of the audience. The pleasure of the spectators is much enhanced by the performances of an excellent orchestra, and the introduction of appropriate songs and ballads by a good company of vocalists.[70]

The large platform was also suitable for what had been the Music Hall's other great money-spinner – the minstrel shows. The famous Christy Minstrels had first visited Sheffield in 1859. By the time the Albert Hall opened the whole country appears to have gone minstrel mad and the Sheffield public was as enthusiastic as ever. One of the first troupes to appear there were Tute's Great Christy Minstrels who came to Barker's Pool in December 1874. Over the next thirty years they were followed by the Christys, the Female Christys, and the Caledonian Minstrels ('fourteen braw men and bonnie lasses'). A local troupe run by Sam Hague, 'The Original Slave Troupe,' was particularly popular as were Matthew's Minstrels, both drawing crowds two thousand strong.

Other popular acts which found their way from Surrey Street to the Albert Hall included Herr Dobler 'The Great Wizard of the Age', and the Spectral Opera Company 'with the famous Pepper's Ghost Illusion' – both did well in their new venue.

The evangelists Sankey and Moody see in the New Year

By far the largest audience to be assembled at the Albert Hall gathered to hear the famous American evangelists Dwight L Moody and Ira D Sankey at their midnight service on 31 December, 1874. The local press described the scene:

> What a noise all these people made, scrambling and shouting as if they were on an excursion platform, or at a theatre on a pantomime night. Their mingled voices sounded louder than the surge of an angry sea, and people in the gallery struggled with more persistency than the restless waves to get to the front, until the crowd became so great that further struggling was impossible, because the arms of the would-be combatants were pinioned by the crush of the multitude.[71]

Their popularity grew and in the end the Albert Hall was overwhelmed. At a service specially for women, 'so great was the crowd, both inside and outside the hall, that Mr Moody left the building and held a service in the Parish Church yard. There had been great crowds since, but nothing to equal the fighting, surging crowd of females who then clamoured for admittance.'[72]

Sankey and Moody caused quite a stir

The army could always be relied on to do its bit for Sheffield's cultural activities and now lent its support to the new hall. At a concert in November 1875, the Band of the Hallamshire Rifles played 'a choice selection of High Class Music'. This included the 'Inauguration March' which had been written by their bandmaster, J M Fordie, for the opening of Firth Park by the Prince and Princess of Wales.

The Royal Hand-Bell Ringers from London also gave what was described as 'a very clever and pleasing entertainment' under the auspices of the Sheffield Sunday School Band of Hope Union. The Ringers, who had appeared before royalty on several occasions, offered a programme performed earlier for Queen Victoria and her family at Windsor. Their conductor, Mr D S Miller, reassured everyone that 'There is nothing low or unhealthy in the entertainment, and those who are seeking a night's pure enjoyment cannot do better than visit the Albert Hall this evening'.[73] It is hard to see how a group of handbell ringers, sponsored by the Band of Hope, could have upset anyone – even in Sheffield!

Finances start to go downhill

There was still a pressing need for further investment to improve the sightlines from the balcony, provide extra doors to combat draughts and complete the decorations – these alone would cost at least a thousand pounds. To make matters worse, income from annual rentals was beginning to fall. In 1874, the first full year of operation, this had amounted to £2,400, but it had been steadily falling since then. By 1875, income had dropped to £1,800 and further reductions were forecast. Not surprisingly investors who had reluctantly put up cash for the new hall were demanding a return and following the annual shareholders meeting, the Company felt obliged to declare a dividend of 3 per cent, leaving little for the much needed improvements. One lone voice, a Mr Gainsford, had pointed out that Sheffield was about the only town which had never offered first class concerts. He had suggested that it might be possible for the directors to introduce a scheme like the one in Leeds where a contractual arrangement with Charles Hallé to provide a series of orchestral concerts had been very successful for several years. But this was Sheffield, not Leeds, and his proposal had fallen on deaf ears.

People's Concerts, Oratorios and Anton Rubenstein

Early in 1876 the first of a series of low-priced People's Concerts was arranged and conducted by John Peck. These were held on Saturday afternoons and occasionally the Mayor, the Master Cutler and other local dignitaries would attend but even with prices as low as one shilling, and three

120

pence for the gallery, the hall was never full – and a second series some years later fared no better. Charles Harvey also put on a few subscription concerts but for the most part it was the other activities which kept the Albert Hall going.

But the proprietors did not lose hope and decided to cash in on the town's enthusiasm for oratorios. In 1877 the 'Albert Choral Society' of about 100 voices was formed by Mr Trimsell, supported by 'a committee of gentlemen'.[74] To the proprietors' delight, Arthur Sullivan's *The Prodigal Son* and *The Light of the World*, performed in Sheffield for the first time, drew in large crowds – and a Children's Concert of five hundred voices managed to fill the hall even at a top price of five shillings.[75] They also confidently expected that Handel's *Messiah* would guarantee a capacity audience at Christmas.

As well as *Messiah,* Christmas shows of a rather more secular nature were staged to compete with the pantomimes at the Royal and the Alexandra. One of these was the 'Blondinette Melodists, the Greatest Company of Lady Artistes in the World, with Lady Instrumentalists, Lady Comediennes and Lady Singers.' Their show included a 'specially written Allegory of the Day' entitled 'Queen or Empress?' discussing the topical proposal that Queen Victoria should become Empress of India.

Anton Rubinstein, the internationally acclaimed Russian pianist and composer, had come to the Albert Hall in March 1877 and there were high hopes that his concert would be sold out. Sadly this was not the case. Once again the audience was small and the local press ignored the performance completely. Rubinstein's third visit was more successful but it seems that on the whole Sheffield audiences still remained lukewarm towards serious music, even to recitals by world famous musicians.

Anton Rubinstein

In 1878, however, the sixty five performers of Gilmore's American Band had a much better reception. This was the band of the 22nd Regiment, New York which was on a European tour prior to appearances at the Paris Exhibition. After successful concerts at the Albert Hall, the band went on to Manchester and then back to Rotherham. On their way, they were greeted at Sheffield station by the American Consul and the Band of the Rotherham Volunteers who played the 'Star Spangled Banner' as the train drew in.

The Albert Hall Lights up

After the summer closure there was just one event of note when another 'American' Henry M Stanley, African explorer and the man who found Doctor Livingstone, lectured to a full hall on 'Through the Dark Continent'.[*] Then, on 21 November, the Albert Hall became the first Sheffield theatrical venue to enjoy the use of electric light. When Federic Maccabe came with his popular show, *Begone Dull Care*, the Albert Hall was illuminated, inside and out, by electric light. Streets and squares in Paris were already lit by

---

[*] Stanley was actually born in Wales but went to America at the age of eighteen and from then on presented himself as an American.

electricity and Maccabe's show was billed as 'The latest Parisian Sensation'. Sheffielders were intrigued:

> A considerable number of persons assembled outside the Albert Hall last evening, attracted by the announcement that the electric light would be displayed from the exterior of the building as well as in the hall during the entertainments given by Mr Frederic Maccabe. Three globes over the portico contained the Jablochkoff candles which were to illuminate the street, and in the hall three large globes were disposed on the platform.

> The engine is concealed somewhere in the dim recesses under the building, where, quite out of the way, it will be fully competent to fulfil the duties expected of it. Owing to an unfortunate accident to the electric machine, the light did not come off very well. It was induced for a time to act, and even under the disadvantageous circumstances in which it was placed it contrasted very favourably with the dull, dirty, yellow flame of the gas in the neighbouring lamps. The light came out white and clear, and was even dispossessed of its somewhat supernatural surroundings in the shape of ghostly blue tint which generally accompanies it. As to its success in the hall, it would be unfair to pronounce an opinion, but there seems every probability that it may be made thoroughly effective for the purposes of modern illumination.[76]

But this was the Albert Hall – built and run on the cheap and Maccabe's innovation was short-lived. Fifteen years later, when the City Theatre opened in a blaze of electric light, the Albert Hall was still lit by gas.

A Vital Spark at the Albert Hall

Financially things were beginning to look up. In their annual report for 1878 the proprietors announced that income from letting the hall had risen from £1,315 in 1877 to £1,561 in 1878 and were sufficiently encouraged to declare a dividend of twelve shillings per share. But the aim to bring a little culture to Sheffield's middle classes was still very much wide of the mark. From 1879 onwards the main attractions followed the same pattern – dioramas, minstrel shows, ballad concerts, and local amateur choral performances including the traditional *Messiah* every Christmas. For some of the popular Albert Hall shows, special trains ran to Sheffield from several surrounding towns, returning at 11.15 pm.

Those concerned with the decline in the quality of entertainment must have been alarmed by an announcement that a famous music hall performer, Miss Jenny Hill was planning a show. The 'Vital Spark' as she was known had been playing the principal boy in *Robinson Crusoe* for the Royal's 1886/7 pantomime season but music hall was her first love and she wanted Sheffield people to see her doing what she did best. So in March 1887 she assembled a supporting music hall company, booked the Albert Hall, and opened on the Monday after the final curtain dropped on the pantomime.

"'ARRY"

SUNG WITH GREAT SUCCESS BY
MISS JENNY HILL,
WRITTEN & COMPOSED BY
E. V. PAGE.
LONDON: WILLEY & C? 14A. G? MARLBOROUGH S? W.

Her show was completely sold out and the audiences loved her range of character songs and her strong supporting cast. Jenny re-booked the Hall in November and again the following April for two weeks. She delighted her public as did her company of vocalists, trick cyclists, male impersonators and Irish comedians. Prices were low at one shilling, sixpence, threepence and two shillings for a reservation. Such shows fell far short of Sir John Brown's dream that the Albert Hall would 'instruct and edify and cultivate the taste for entertainments of a refining tendency' but Jenny Hill's success encouraged the proprietors to abandon these lofty ideals and to let the hall to other variety performers.

Little enthusiasm for *The Golden Legend*

Not everyone, however, gave up on the idea of cultivating an audience for classical entertainment.   In 1887, the Sheffield Tonic Sol-fa Association staged Arthur Sullivan's *The Golden Legend,* under the direction Henry Coward, another crusader in the cause of serious music. Although the show was felt to be an artistic triumph, it did not succeed financially and the expensive seats were empty.

The Albert Hall last evening again bore testimony to the lack of appreciation of musical enterprise on the part of the upper class. This is all the more to be regretted when it is known that the Sheffield Tonic Sol-fa Association, which body was responsible for the production of Sir Arthur Sullivan's *Golden Legend*, had spared no expense in carrying out the determination to give the town an opportunity of hearing the leading feature of the last Leeds Festival in the most favourable surroundings.[77]

So for the most part it was back to the usual lowbrow fare – panoramas combined with other acts, 'negro songs and sketches', ventriloquism, acrobatic feats and a troupe of performing Russian bear hounds. However, there was some progress. A series of low-priced 'popular' Saturday night concerts, promoted by William Brown, were exrtremely successful and became a regular fixture on the Albert Hall calendar for many years.

Eugen Sandow

A German wrestler – Henry Irving and Ellen Terry

In February 1890, the Albert Hall played host to Eugen Sandow, the famous German wrestler and holder of the world's weight-lifting championship title. This was his first provincial tour and people came in droves to see his show which included 'Attila the accomplished athlete', 'Bertram the Bewilderer', a magician, the 'Blue Hungarian Band with their Wild Weird Melodies', and Sandow himself in a novel illustration of 'Muscle, Music and Mystery'. It was a sell-out for all three days at three shillings, two shillings, one shilling, and sixpence.

125

But at last interest in more serious entertainment was growing. In June, after an absence of eleven years, Henry Irving came to the hall with Ellen Terry. They took a chance and defied theatrical superstition by giving a reading of *Macbeth* – on Friday the thirteenth. It was rather an odd evening. The couple stood at separate desks with massive copies of a text prepared by Irving. He wore evening dress, she wore a white Grecian-style gown. Some of Shakespeare's characters had been eliminated, others reduced in importance and much of the text was condensed. Despite all this the large audience was enthusiastic and they loved the music, specially composed by Arthur Sullivan.

Sir Charles Hallé, Adelina Patti, Joachim and Paderewski

Classical performances were also beginning to find a larger audience and in 1889 the recently knighted Sir Charles Hallé put on a highly successful concert featuring Sims Reeves. Even the five shilling seats were sold out for this one! In November a return visit by Adelina Patti, 'Prima Donna of the World', was also a sell-out. Sheffield had waited a long time for a second chance to hear this remarkable voice. It was twenty-seven years since, at the age of eighteen, she had appeared at the Music Hall in Surrey Street. Sheffield's smart set turned out in force.

> The hall presented a memorable sight, there being such a collection of fashion and influence as is seldom seen in Sheffield; in fact it seemed as though it were some state occasion so many important families and town dignatories were present.[78]

Now that the Albert Hall had at last become an established venue for serious music, the number of classical concerts and recitals increased. The Hallé Orchestra, as it was now styled, finally became a box office success and Miss E L McKnight became the first woman to play the magnificent organ. There were more concerts by Adelina Patti and whenever the Queen of Song appeared, there was standing room only, and the top price was fifteen shillings.[*]

Famous European artists such as the outstanding violinist Joseph Joachim and the brilliant Polish pianist Paderewski also attracted huge audiences. The local press noted that it was remarkable that so many

---

[*] Patti's agents were quick to deny allegations that she had been dissatisfied with the receipts from her previous visit.

Sheffield people had been prepared to pay high prices for Paderewski's recital, double those charged for Rubinstein whose first concert in the town had been so very poorly attended.[79]

Necessary improvements as the century draws to a close

The 1880s had seen the start of a drive by the local authorities to improve safety in the town's public buildings. An inspection by the magistrates revealed that the Albert Hall did not measure up to the new

World Class performers at the Albert Hall

Joseph Joachim   *Jan Paderewski*

standards and it was decided that wider staircases must be provided to meet the new fire escape requirements. The proprietors were dismayed by the estimated cost of £2,800 but they had little choice. If they did not comply, the Hall would have to close. So the alterations went ahead and by 1890 the building was one of the safest places of entertainment in the country.

In 1893 the Albert Hall was twenty years old. The big ugly building had never quite lived up to expectations but had provided some decent musical entertainment and, by being prepared to pander to popular taste, had managed to remain a viable proposition. But 1893 was the year when the shareholders made the huge mistake. Even though some of the town's streets had been lit by electricity for over two years and the new theatre in Tudor Street had electric lights on both sides of the curtain, the shareholders voted to spend money on draught-proofing instead.

From the eighteen nineties onwards the hall became increasingly involved in showing motion pictures. Eventually it was taken over by New Century Pictures which in turn became part of the Gaumont British Picture Corporation. It opened as the Gaumont in 1927.

Part 4
And the Rest -
Something for Everyone

As the century wore on Sheffield's population and prosperity grew and the demand for entertainment increased. The two main theatres, the concert halls and the many music halls did not always provide what was wanted. However, there were alternatives. New attractions appeared in a wide variety of public buildings, new halls were built to cater for more discerning audiences and travelling circuses provided family entertainment. In the summer, there were elaborate, open-air performances in Sheffield's gardens.

129

Circuses and Travelling Shows

During the Georgian period, travelling circuses and equestrian shows had provided serious competition for the Theatre in Tudor Street and they remained hugely popular during Victoria's reign. The townsfolk may have been luke-warm in their appreciation of drama and high-class musical entertainment but their enthusiasm for circuses knew no bounds. This was perhaps not surprising since, unlike the proprietors of the Theatre Royal, the circus owners spent a great deal of money on providing spectacular venues and the town attracted some of the best shows on the road – Charles Hengler, John and George Sanger, Charles Adams and even the legendary Buffalo Bill all came to Sheffield.

Essentially these were horse shows with the equestrian turns supported by acrobats, tumblers, gymnasts and clowns. But the circuses were very willing to adapt by bringing in speciality acts and, around Christmas time, pantomime-style entertainment began to feature regularly in their programmes. The mainstream theatres were far from happy about this but there seems to have been little they could do for circuses were extremely popular.

The circuses usually performed in huge, temporary wooden buildings, well-appointed with good seating and elaborate décor matching that of the permanent theatres. Prices were not particularly cheap. Indeed an evening at the circus could cost as much as three or four shillings – about the same as an evening at the Royal – but these touring shows seem to find little difficulty in attracting big audiences from all levels of society.

Most circus owners were drawn to vacant lots near the former Victoria Railway Station where there was plenty of space for their temporary encampments. There were occasional performances in Duke Street[*] in the town centre and some circuses took advantage of the site in Barker's Pool which had been cleared for the future Albert Hall. But it was not until 1888 that the Sanger Brothers developed a large permanent site between Pinstone Street and Union Street. This massive wooden structure which, apart from the circus ring in front of the stage, had all the appearance of a traditional

---

[*] Off The Moor, later renamed Matilda Street.

130

theatre, was said to be the largest of its kind in the country. It remained in continuous use until 1895 when the Empire Theatre opened.

Hengler's Circus

On 4 April 1859, Charles Hengler, one of the greatest names in the nineteenth-century circus world, brought his Grand Cirque Varieté to Duke Street. Later he recouped his costs by renting out his wooden building to other circuses – McCollum's Grand Anglo-Saxon Circus (from the Royal Alhambra Palace, Leicester Square, London), Frowde's Cirque Modèle, Franconia's Grand Champs Elysees Cirque and Ginnetts' Mammoth Circus.

Hengler's visit to Sheffield in October 1872 was blighted by a frightening incident. This time he occupied a custom-built wooden building in Station Road, elegantly upholstered and brilliantly lit but after only a couple of weeks the performance was brought to an abrupt stop when a wall at the back of the gallery suddenly collapsed. Some fifty members of the audience, including children, suffered serious injuries. Hengler, jealous of his excellent reputation for safety, made special arrangements for a doctor to visit them. Despite this show of concern, however, the circus was up and running to good audiences within a few days.[80] It was only after a hugely successful Christmas programme that the Grand Cirque moved on and the patched-up structure was removed.

Sangers' Circus lights up Sheffield

'Lord' George Sanger

'Lord' John Sanger

131

Sanger Brothers' Great International Circus, perhaps the most famous of all nineteenth-century circuses, came to Sheffield in November 1862 and spent about ten weeks in an enormous wooden structure near the Station. The building was divided, theatre fashion, into stalls, boxes, pit, and gallery, known as the promenade, where smoking was permitted. All this was brightly lit by fifty gasoliers and six crystal chandeliers decorated with bouquets of glass flowers.

The appeal of pantomime at the Theatre Royal encouraged the brothers to offer *Blue Beard! or, A Merry Christmas Festival in Sheffield* at Christmas 1863 which enjoyed a successful run, despite efforts by Charles Pitt to close it down.[*] Keen to maintain their popularity, they treated the local workhouse children to a free performance, a piece of cake, a glass of wine and sweets. They also staged two benefit performances one for Sheffield Royal Infirmary and the other for the widows and orphans of miners killed in the recent accident at Edmund's Main Colliery.

The Sangers made regular highly successful visits over the next twenty years and in 1888 they built their huge Royal Hippodrome in the city centre. The first show opened on 12 November. The entire company marched in procession from the Victoria Station to Pinstone Street with ten elephants, a hundred and twenty horses and ponies, camels, dromedaries, llamas, baboons and kangaroos. At Christmas a 'Grand Seasonable Spectacle' offered a *Carnival on the Ice, or, A Night in St Petersburg.* It was to all intents and purposes a pantomime and the show drew record crowds. The *Independent* was particularly delighted by the inclusion of a harlequinade which in recent years had fallen out of fashion:

> . . . . young people who want to know what their fathers laughed at in the days of Joseph Grimaldi should certainly see the harlequinade in Sanger's arena. Those who can appreciate a clever and novel entertainment, and enjoy a hearty laugh at witticism without a trace of vulgarity, will certainly include Sanger's hippodrome in the places to be visited during the holidays.[81]

At the 1890 show, ice gave way to water and the whole circus ring was submerged under 25,000 gallons for *The Pantomime on the Water.* There was a special matinee for charity children – 'The Little Waifs of the Sheffield Robin Club'. The following winter, the pantomime programme included a

---

[*] See page 20.

speciality turn, 'St Joan of Arc on Horseback', as well as performing lions, 'Thora, the lady ladder ascensionist' and a re-enactment of the topical Zulu War. 'Lord' John Sanger and 'Lord' George Sanger never did things by halves.[*] Seats were considerably cheaper than those of rival circuses – you could see the show for threepence and the best seats only cost a shilling.

Sam Lockhart comes at Christmas

Sam Lockhart's Circus replaced Sangers' for the 1892 Christmas show and offered a pantomime *Nicodemus, or, the Green Demons and the Good Fairy Green, Beauty and Grace,* featuring a spectacular transformation scene behind a screen of fireworks. Excellent notices in the Press helped to improve on a slow start but times were hard and Sam Lockhart was back on the road sooner than expected.

Sam Lockhart and friend

Quaglieni's Italian Circus

There were plenty of other circuses besides those of Hengler and the Sanger brothers. Antonio Quaglieni first brought his Italian Circus to Sheffield in 1868 and returned twice, using the sites in Duke Street and Barker's Pool. These temporary buildings were quite elaborate with good heating and excellent lighting. In Duke Street more than four hundred and seventy gas jets were mounted on the capitals of the supporting pillars and a 'circle of light, thirty feet in diameter' was installed above the ring. David Seal, a 'Shakespearean jester,' was praised for providing humour 'in a manner that was remarkable for its freedom from anything like vulgarity' and there were plenty of thrilling acts. One of Sheffield's favourite spectacles, *Mazeppa or The Wild Horse of Tartary*, was a regular feature of

---

[*] John Sanger and his brother George changed their names by deed poll to 'Lord John Sanger' and 'Lord George Sanger'.

133

Quaglieni's Italian Circus and on St George's Day audiences were treated to an equestrian show featuring St George and the Dragon.

Charles Adams' Grand Circus

In 1874, Sheffield's enthusiasm for circuses encouraged Charles Adams to winter his large travelling show on the old Hengler site during the dark winter months. Adams' prefabricated building was impressive. Its huge roof was supported by no fewer than eleven pillars complete with Corinthian capitals and it could accommodate an audience of 3,000. Once again the glittering interior was in sharp contrast with some of the town's other, more permanent places of entertainment so a visit to the circus was quite a thrilling experience even before the show started. The *Independent* commented that 'Mr Adams' establishment will be a most attractive addition to our other places of amusement.'[82]

On gala nights the show was graced by civic dignitaries and whenever a local army band performed, one of their top brass came along. Special features included Old English Rural sports (complete with fox hunt), a steeplechase, and Dick Turpin's Ride to York On Black Bess which always brought the house down. Despite relatively high prices Adams' circus managed to attract big audiences.

Newsome's Circus

James Newsome brought his circus in 1877. An elaborate octagonal building was constructed near the Station – seating 2,500 plus a promenade area. The entrance to the expensive seats was lit by chandeliers and the main auditorium had a dome-like roof above the forty-two foot diameter circus ring, brightly lit and well ventilated. Faux marble pillars were decorated with statues, shields and flags, and the capitals were festooned with drapery. Mindful of Hengler's accident, the advertisements stressed that the building had been 'certified by the Borough surveyor, Mr P B Coghlan, as to its perfect stability'.

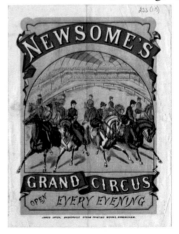

134

The spectacular Christmas show, *Dick Whittington and Cat*, featured the 'star of the clowns, Little Meers' as the cat and, as a highlight, *The Fairies Banquet and Miniature Lord Mayor's Show* transformed the ring 'into a noble and spacious banqueting hall with Gothic furniture in white and gold. The floor was laid with a magnificent carpet of artistic design representing a tessellated pavement.'[83]

Keith's New Circus

Charlie Keith

Another purpose-built construction near the station, was occupied by Keith's New Circus for the month of February 1883. In the final week about a hundred local children took part in *Little Red Riding Hood* which also featured a patriotic parade of soldiers 'newly returned from the Egyptian campaign'– some were even 'decorated' by a member of the company posing as Queen Victoria. The press reported that the event was 'crowded in every part' and that 'many persons were unable to obtain admission.'[84]

Buffalo Bill and Annie Oakley ride into town

William F Cody, Buffalo Bill, was one of those rare people who became a legend in their own lifetime. Indeed his exploits took on an almost mythological significance in the romantic story of the American West. And he came to Sheffield. Buffalo Bill's Wild West Show visited the town in August 1891.

A suitable site was found for his huge company near the Hillsborough tram terminus. The company arrived at Wadsley Bridge Station in three special trains consisting of seventy-three carriages and trucks. Unfortunately, the weather was terrible and advance bookings were not very promising. Buffalo Bill, claiming to be 'specially desirous of pleasing the Sheffield artisans', decided to lead his entire company on a march through the streets. It worked. The big parade drew over a hundred thousand people and several thousand attended the opening night.

There were two performances each day, at three in the afternoon and eight in the evening. Ticket prices were high – a shilling for the cheapest

135

seats, four shillings for the most expensive, protected from the weather. Everyone agreed that it was a magnificent show, especially the shooting and riding by Buffalo Bill and the famous Miss Annie Oakley. The climax came with an 'Indian attack on the Deadwood mail coach and the rescue of the passengers by Buffalo Bill and a band of cowboys' – well worth the entrance fee.[85]

Sharp shooters Buffalo Bill and Annie Oakley

Sadly, Buffalo Bill's visit to Sheffield was marred by a terrible accident. Paul Eagle Star, a member of the Sioux tribe, was injured when his horse fell under him and his right leg became trapped against the entrance to the ring. He was rushed to Sheffield Royal Infirmary where his right leg was amputated but he did not survive the shock of the operation and died eight days later.[86]

The Grand Circus

In 1879, Charles Weldon attempted to set up a permanent circus on an excellent central location, right opposite the Theatre Royal, but the project failed and after a few months the ring was boarded over and the building was used as a large music hall.[*]

---

[*] Because it was a circus for such a short while, we have included details of events at the Grand Circus in the Music Hall section. See pages 86-88.

136

Fairs and travelling menageries – Little Tich and Wombwell

Entertainment at Sheffield Fair was rarely mentioned by the Press and usually only when there was a disaster of some kind. On 2 December, 1854 the *Independent* reported that 'the wind played disastrous havoc with the

slender tents. Stacey's theatre booth was so far dismantled and tumbled down that it could not be re-erected for performances the following day.' But fairs were able to pay good money and high class entertainment was sometimes to be found there. The Whitsuntide Fair of June, 1892 included Randell Williams' Great Ghost Show, of which 'the front alone cost £1,000.' This was housed in a large temporary wooden theatre with 4,800 seats. The star of the show was the famous 'Little Tich' – and his enormous feet.

Little Titch

Sangers' Circus was not the only place in Sheffield to display wild and exotic animals from other countries. Throughout the nineteenth century there were a number of itinerant zoos which carted a variety of animals around the country and gave people the opportunity to see lions, tigers and other dangerous animals at close quarters. Wombwell's Menagerie, one of the oldest and biggest of these travelling shows, was a regular visitor to Sheffield throughout the Victorian period.

Wombwell regularly brought fifteen wagons full of animals to Sheffield

The Gardens

The Botanical Gardens

On a fine day in Victorian Sheffield what could be better than a visit to one of the gardens dotted about the town to see what was on offer by way of entertainment – for in the summer months these gardens would open their gates and put on a show. There were some wonderfully spectacular events and high class acts. Music hall artists could be found performing in the afternoon, supplementing their regular income as well as gaining free publicity. These popular open-air events often attracted several thousand spectators.

Unfortunately, many of these places were not open for long. The rapid growth of trade and industry began to swallow up any undeveloped sites and parks and gardens were often commandeered to provide housing for the ever-expanding workforce.

Exciting times at the Botanical Gardens

The Botanical Gardens which opened on Clarkhouse Road in 1836 are the only one of Sheffield's many Victorian gardens to survive to the present day.[*] Entrance was normally restricted to shareholders and subscribers but about four times a year, on special gala days, the Gardens were thrown open to the general public.

Blondin made regular visits to Sheffield

All kinds of amusements could be found there, including a bear pit. The band of the 4th West Yorkshire Artillery Volunteers and the Norfolk Park Band performed light orchestral concerts and there were appearances by top class entertainers. In the early 1860s the tight-rope walker Charles Blondin made his first visit to the town, not long after his famous walk across the Niagara Falls.[**] He obviously felt at home in Sheffield for he returned many times and made his final visit in 1893, still defying gravity at the age of sixty-nine. There were other impressive performances. The New Zealand Chiefs demonstrated Maori modes of warfare, songs and war dances and another top-notch performer, Sam Collins, delighted a huge crowd with his music hall act.[***]

The highlight of the Botanical Gardens' year were the Whitsuntide galas. The programme for Whit Monday in 1863 gives us a good idea of the wide variety of the entertainment on offer. The 'People's Festival' included three different bands – the Band of the 8th King's Regiment, the Chesterfield Brass Band and the Sheffield Artillery Band. A 'Grand Military Entertainment' was presented with an 'Assault at Arms devised by Professor Gregory' – and he brought along Master Gregory, 'Infant Gymnast', who performed an Indian Club Exercise. There was also a demonstration of Old English Quarter-Staff fighting, 'Feats of Swordsmanship', some performing dogs, the 'American Troupe of Birds', the 'Stereorama', air gun shooting, and a Montgolfier balloon ascent. As if these were not enough there was a 'Cupid's Post Office' and dancing on a

---

[*] After years of neglect the gardens underwent a major programme of restoration during the late 1990s and are still used for cultural events.
[**] Blondin was not actually called Charles. His full name was Jean François Gravelet Blondin.
[***] Reported in the *Independent* of 22.8.1863. Collins' name was preserved in London's Collins Music Hall which opened in 1863 and finally closed in 1958.

special pre-fabricated wooden floor accompanied by a string band. You could have had all this for sixpence – or threepence if you happened to be under twelve! The Whitsun gala of 1865 featured musical sketches by the Savannah Minstrels, an original Ethiopean Burlesque and 'Terpsichorian' Entertainments by Lallah and Signor Verdi. In 1891, the veteran hot-air balloonist, Mr Lythgoe, made an ascent accompanied by Mrs Whelan. Some of the nine thousand spectators followed the balloon on foot as it drifted westward. It landed at Dore Moor.

Cremorne Gardens, Highfields

Cremorne, a large private house, opened its beautiful gardens to the public in the 1850s following the death of the owner, Mr T Tillotson. They were fairly close to the town centre and offered a welcome relief from the smoke and grime of the Sheffield streets. An advertisement in the *Independent* of 31 May, 1862 describes Cremorne as

> The most beautiful and extensive gardens in the Kingdom. Extraordinary novelties to be introduced during the season. An omnibus will leave the Newmarket at 2 p.m. and run every hour up to 9 p.m.

On three occasions during the summer of 1862, a crowd of between ten and fifteen thousand people watched Blondin's daring acrobatic tricks on a tightrope 68 feet high and 360 feet long. The spectacular show was rounded off by a firework display. On each occasion, the weather was unusually kind and when the great star arrived from London for his second appearance, he was greeted by a band and conveyed to Cremorne Gardens in a carriage drawn by four greys.

In July that year, Mr Warhurst the proprietor announced another 'Grand Array of Talent! Novelty Trips the Heels of Novelty!' for his Grand Gala of Monday, 28 July, 1862. He had, he said,

> secured the services of the renowned **MONS. KEMP**, the only Rival of the Great and Glorious **LEOTARD**, whose perilous performances on the **FLYING TRAPEZE** has astonished thousands of spectators. His daring and most astounding Feats, performed in mid-air and with as much ease as when a bird takes wing, must be seen to be appreciated, as no description can give an adequate idea of the nature of these truly marvellous performances...**THE BROTHERS TRAVIS**, Champion Dancers, and Celebrated Delineators of Nigger Life in Old Kentucky, will on this occasion perform some of the choicest and most popular

pieces of Negro Melodies, and will exhibit to the admirers of Terpsichorean Art an exhibition of skill in Lancashire Clog and Boot Dancing, never before witnessed in Sheffield.

There were other quite strange 'gala' events at Cremorne. A 'Monster Gathering' of two thousand old ladies (aged upwards of fifty years!), admitted free of charge, were given tea and entertained by 'the time honoured dance of Sir Roger de Coverley performed by twenty of the oldest ladies'. There was also a most unusual cricket match between a one-legged eleven and a one-armed eleven. All the players in this bizarre event were military and naval pensioners.

But Cremorne was not a very profitable enterprise. In 1866, its name was changed to the Orphanage and, although it kept going for a few more months, it was not long before it was sold for property development. The Cremorne public house in London Road is all that is left to remind us of the 'most beautiful and extensive gardens in the Kingdom'.

Newhall Gardens

New Hall, a mansion in the Attercliffe area, stood in twenty two acres of ornamental grounds and paddocks. John Sanderson, the last private owner of the estate, died in 1853 and like Cremorne, the gardens at New Hall became an outdoor pleasure park offering various attractions including races, cricket, and other sporting events. Circuses and equestrian shows were also regular visitors. The house itself provided refreshment and billiard rooms and, on occasion, doubled as a grandstand.

The gardens opened on 1 May, 1854 with a 'Grand Cricket Match between the United Eleven of All England and the Fifteen of Sheffield' followed in June by Pablo Fanque's equestrian show. Despite a poor bus service and its distance from the Brightside station, the park quickly became a going concern with some fifty thousand visitors each week. The gardens were spruced up, the derelict maze and bowling green were restored, and the first season ended with a grand fete on 2 October.

Pablo Fanque

141

There was currently a huge interest in the events of the Crimean War and the storming of Odessa was the centerpiece of a splendid firework display.

On 25 June, Thomas Youdan mounted a charity show in aid of the Licenced Victuallers Asylum at Grimesthorpe. It went well and the following year he repeated the event on an even larger scale with three bands and the entire company from his Surrey Music Hall. The balloon ascent by 'Mr Coxwell in his celebrated war balloon' remained airborne for about an hour and eventually landed near Doncaster. The day ended with a grand display of fireworks watched by a crowd of twelve thousand and Youdan was able to donate £300 to the Crimean War Memorial fund.

Youdan was not the only music hall proprietor to make use of these attractive grounds – Thomas Jackson, who ran the Royal Pavilion Music Hall next door to the Royal, also put on shows there. Starring in one of these was the ubiquitous Mrs Ramsden and her 'highly-trained troupe of twenty children' who gave a 'Scottish musical terpsichorean spectacle entitled The Gathering of the Clans'. An even bigger attraction was a visit by Blondin, a couple of months before he appeared at Cremorne Gardens. He performed his high-wire act before a crowd of ten thousand – some arriving by special trains from as far away as Birmingham.

The exciting and highly profitable events of the early years did not last and the land was gradually sold off for building development. The final thirteen acres disappeared in October 1891.

All that is left –   the Cremorne and Sheaf House public houses

Sheaf House Gardens

The ornamental gardens at Sheaf House on Bramall Lane opened towards the end of the 1860s. For the price of sixpence, varied amusements were on offer such as those advertised on 19 June, 1871. Patrons were promised the usual funfair attractions. These included:

Dancing to two splendid bands;
The wondrous Bellina troupe (six in number);
Mons. Ballandino, King of the High Wire.
This artiste turns 200 somersaults in mid air;
Monsieur Eugeny, the Great Fire Prince,
on the high rope enveloped in flames;
Arthur and Ella, duettists and favourite ballads
Bob Gordon, the original Funny Man;
Mademoiselle Serino, see her great Can-Can Dance in Mid Air;
and Timmy Bubble, the funny and original clown.

Blondin himself did not appear at Sheaf House but the 'Renowned African Blondin, Son of the Desert, on the High Rope' topped the bill on Whit Monday, 1872. In 1876, a team consisting of actors from the two Christmas pantomimes played a charity match against the Garrick Football Club at Bramall Lane. A huge crowd of about 20,000 turned up and naturally caused quite a bit of damage. The following year, the Lane refused permission to hold the match but all was not lost. The second match, with a slightly smaller and rather better behaved crowd, was played a couple of hundred yards up the road at Sheaf Gardens – this time against a team of Licensed Victuallers. The pantomime team were in full costume and their opponents wore their traditional shirtsleeves and aprons.

The grounds were eventually sold off for housing. Sheaf House, now a pub, still stands in Bramall Lane.

Kelvin Grove

To the north of the town, the grounds of Kelvin Grove provided another open space where relatively low-cost entertainment could be enjoyed. In the 1840s and 1850s the grounds were open every afternoon and evening providing popular concerts and spectacular firework displays. It was only threepence to go in during the afternoon but the price doubled after five o'clock. However, it was not long before the rising tide of bricks and mortar completely engulfed the site and Sheffield lost yet another of its popular open spaces.

Victoria Gardens

By the early 1880s, sites near the centre of Sheffield were disappearing fast and Alderman Joseph Mountain, a developer from Abbeydale, recognising the continuing need for open spaces, created a new recreational park at Totley on the extreme edge of the town. The Gardens occupied a fifteen acre site with a four-hundred yard frontage onto Baslow Road – about fifteen minutes walk from Dore railway station.

As part of his project, Mountain built refreshment pavilions and a ballroom one hundred and eighty feet long by sixty feet wide. He also provided facilities for several kinds of sports, brass band concerts, minstrel shows and all the usual attractions. The Victoria Gardens opened on Whit Monday, 1883 and for many years these gardens provided a popular resort for the townspeople. Easter time 1886 saw around twelve thousand enjoy the fine weather.

The Gardens, an ideal location for balloon ascents and parachute descents seemed to hold a particular attraction for lady performers. On 14 June, 1886 'Mlle de Vasco, the only female astronaut' was the first woman to make a balloon ascent. She was followed in September, 1890 by Miss Maud Brooks of Liverpool who went one better. Not only did she go up in a balloon but made a parachute jump from it at around four thousand feet above the watching crowds. Maud, who was nineteen at the time but looked younger, sported pink tights, a crimson bodice trimmed with lace and a cap of peacock blue with her hair loose to her waist. She wore a string of beads and, amazingly, carried a bouquet. This costume hardly sounds suitable for a parachute jump, but the intrepid Maud landed safely in a field between Totley Brook and Dore Church. Two years later and by this time described as 'England's Original Parachute Queen', Maud made a second jump, dropped over five thousand feet and landed in a field near Unstone. The balloon ended up at Chaddesden near Derby.

But Alderman Mountain's dream could not last for ever and the Victoria Gardens, like so many others, eventually gave way to urban development and became a large residential estate.

144

Halls Great and Small – Other Places of Entertainment

Since open-air performances were strictly limited to the summer months and heavily dependent on good weather, indoor events in halls and public buildings throughout the town were well attended.

Large Halls

A Spectacular *Messiah* at the Corn Exchange

The Corn Exchange, built by the Duke of Norfolk in 1881, was a vast hall close to the site of the present Park Square roundabout. It quickly grew in popularity and a performance of *Messiah* in 1891 gives us an idea of the scope provided by the huge auditorium. The hall was decorated with foliage and flowers, Chinese Lanterns, flags and banners. Hundreds of chairs were brought in and a special platform was erected for an enormous chorus of five hundred singers accompanied by an orchestra of a hundred musicians. Seats were priced at three shillings for a padded chair (two shillings unpadded) and one shilling for the promenade. Eventually, despite its early success, audiences began to drift away from the Exchange to less expensive venues and in later years it was used mainly for boxing matches and other events guaranteed to attract large crowds[*].

Drill Halls in Edmund Road and Glossop Road

What Sheffield's Drill Halls lacked in beauty, they more than made up for in size and were ideal for reasonably priced concerts, balls and equestrian events. The enormous Norfolk Drill Hall in Edmund Road could accommodate an audience of two thousand and the space was large enough for Charles Blondin to perform his entire repertoire there in 1885 – dancing along the rope in gorgeous costumes, carrying his assistant whilst walking blindfold and riding a bicycle.[87] And, in 1889, the huge hall housed a twenty-hour ladies' bicycle race.

The building was demolished in 1964 following bomb damage in the second world war and a serious fire in 1947.

LADY BICYCLISTS AT THE DRILL HALL

Holiday makers in search of a novelty cannot do better than pay a visit to the Artillery Drill Hall, where there is at present in progress a twenty-hour ladies' bicycle race. The competitors, it need hardly be stated, hail from the land of the Stars and Stripes, where such contests are no new thing.

£75, divided into three prizes of £40, £25 and £10, will be awarded to the three ladies covering the greatest distance within the time stated, and as the fair cyclists have each achieved records, and an excellent race may be anticipated.

The contestants are five in number. Miss Jessie Wood, who is a native of London, is 17 years of age, and holds the 24-hour ladies' world record, made in Omaha, U.S.A. She accomplished 356 miles.

Miss Lottie Stanley, of Pittsburg, U.S.A., is 18 years of age, and the 48-hour champion of the world, and the holder of the *Police Gazette* medal with a record of 679 miles. She is also the only holder of an English long-distance record, having won the 18 hour race at Sunderland with 269 3/4 miles.

Miss Louisa Amiaindo, of Montreal, Canada, is 27 years of age, and is stated to be the oldest professional rider in the world. She is the possessor of the long-distance six-days' championship, with a record of 1000 miles, having defeated such well-known professional cyclists as Woodside and Morgan.

Miss May Allen, 17 years of age, is a native of Philadelphia, and has also accomplished some good performances, and whilst at Sunderland she exhibited her pluck by riding 100 miles with a broken arm.

The last of the number is Miss Lillie Williams, of Omaha, U.S.A., who is 21 years of age, and is the holder of the U.S. 18 hour record and championship. It is noteworthy that she won the first professional race she entered.

There was not a very large attendance at the Drill Hall on Christmas Eve to see the commencement of the race, but as it grows in interest the number of spectators is sure to be largely increased. The five were started at half-past six, and at the call of time - four hours later - the following distances had been made:- Miss Stanley, 57 miles 1 lap; Miss Allen, 56 miles 8 laps; Miss Amiaindo, 55 miles and Miss Williams and Miss Wood, 52 miles 9 laps each.

Yesterday the competitors rode two hours in the afternoon, and from eight to ten in the evening, in the presence of a large number of spectators. When the gun was fired the distances covered stood as follows: Miss Stanley, 118 miles 4 laps; Miss Allen, 117 miles 2 laps; Miss Wood, 113 miles 8 laps; Miss Amiaindo, 113 miles 5 laps and Miss Williams, 101 miles 6 laps.

Mexican Joe's Wild West Show, a smaller version of Buffalo Bill Cody's circus, spent a month at the Drill Hall. The spectacular programme included Indians, buffalo hunters, American scouts, Texas Rangers and a stagecoach drawn by six horses, all introduced by Mexican Joe (Colonel Joe Shelley).

Towards the end of the tour, to the horror of the audience, Running Wolf, one of the most savage of the troupe, took a shot at his boss, hitting him in the face and causing blood to 'flow rather freely.' Despite this apparent loss of blood, Mexican Joe made a miraculous recovery and was greeted with loud cheers when he reappeared. It was later discovered that a similar 'accident' had occurred in other venues but even so, the publicity filled the hall for the final week and the show returned the following year.

Mexican Joe thrilled audiences at the Drill Hall

There was also more serious entertainment. Sims Reeves, the tenor much loved by local audiences, who had performed many times in the town's concert halls, chose Edmund Road for his final appearance in Sheffield.[88]

The Engineers' Drill Hall in Glossop Road also staged a number of concerts and other events during the 1880s and 1890s. At Christmas, it provided an excellent space for a ballroom which, because of its considerable size, was very suitable for quadrille assemblies.

Cheap concerts at the Bath Saloon

Between 1837 and 1895, The Bath Saloon, above the swimming baths on Glossop Road, became a popular venue for concerts, lectures, dance quadrilles as well as productions by the Sheffield Masonic Amateur Dramatic Society and the Sheffield Amateur Dramatic Society. In April 1857, the *Independent* reported that ten shillings would provide for 'three persons to attend no less than five concerts'. But, as so often happens, prices began to creep up, and by 1878, the regular 'soirées musicales' cost three shillings and sixpence per ticket. In 1895, the Baths were sold by auction and completely rebuilt – but the Saloon was not replaced.

147

Temperance Halls and Vestry Halls

For those who did not feel at home in the upmarket theatres and concert halls and who shunned the boozy music halls and public houses, the temperance halls which sprang up in the middle of the nineteenth century provided an inexpensive and enjoyable evening out. No alcohol was permitted and it was hoped to lure members of the working class away from West Bar to enjoy wholesome entertainment with not a drink, or a drunk, in sight. The highest prices were no more than a shilling and many seats could be had for as little as two or three pence.

Acts and lectures were tailored to suit the tastes of temperate audiences. Panoramas and minstrel shows were considered acceptable as was entertainment by local and visiting choirs. Social concerns of the time were reflected in performances of 'Uncle Tom's Cabin' by The Pennsylvania Jubilee Singers and 'Early Closing Association evenings' raised funds 'to improve the lot of shopworkers'. Much amusement was derived from displays by mesmerists and phrenologists in the guise of scientific experiments to satisfy 'instructional and educational needs' of the rather puritanical audiences. Professor Balme, self-styled King of Mesmerists, kept his audience in fits of laughter at the antics of hapless volunteers cavorting under his hypnotic control. More important and serious lessons, however, were learned from an exhibition in 1856 of 350 photographs of the Crimean War, by Roger Fenton, which offered for the first time a vivid pictorial account of the horrors of a military campaign.

Tending the wounded

148

There were three temperance halls in Sheffield of which the most impressive was situated in Townhead Street. This was launched on 5 February, 1856, with seating for two thousand, and despite early financial problems, became a great success. By 1880 things were going so well that £300 was invested in a complete refurbishment, giving the hall 'an elegant

and attractive appearance'. Features included faux marble pillars with gold capitals, statues of gods and goddesses, Italian decor and sculptured friezes. Brilliant lighting was provided by large chandeliers and light brackets 'of twisted brass of new design' and a highly efficient ventilation system was installed.

The Temperance Hall became The Playhouse

Some fifty years later, the Hall took on the status of a regular theatre, was re-named The Sheffield Playhouse and became the home of the Sheffield Repertory Company. It did not finally close until 1971 when the Playhouse was replaced by the Crucible Theatre.

The other Temperance Halls on Barker's Pool and Ellesmere Road were more modest affairs. The Barker's Pool Hall opened in 1855 and closed just seven years later, and the Hall in Ellesmere Road offered cheap and cheerful Grand Miscellaneous Entertainments with songs, glees, solos, recitations and dialogues, presided over by a music hall-style chairman.

Respectable entertainment for a few pence was also provided on a smaller scale at the Vestry Halls, the public buildings used primarily for local administrative matters.* The Vestry Hall in West Bar where Youdan's Surrey Music Hall once stood, bang in the middle of a sea of seedy and sleazy music halls and pubs, could be relied on for an amusing evening out. It opened in 1883 with a series of concerts, competitions and talent contests. Programmes were similar to those found in the Temperance Halls – minstrel shows, panoramas, mesmerists and gaily dressed choirs. The Merry Bohemians, a group founded by J W Cummins, a former leader of the

---

* For example, the Vestry Hall at Burngreave originally accommodated the Brightside Bierlow which was responsible for the administration of the poor law in the area. Bierlow is a dialect word for 'ward' or 'township'.

Sheffield Sunday School Band of Hope, regularly drew full houses with John Jackson, 'the Juvenile Paganini', Herr Karl Zeidler, 'conjuror and ventriloquist' and 'Little Beatrice Benton'. The entertainment concluded with 'Views from each of the Five Continents' projected onto a large screen.

The Vestry Hall in Attercliffe was another popular venue. Concerts arranged by the People's Entertainment Society, a group which aimed to provide low-cost amusement for those who could not afford the theatres and preferred not to frequent the music halls.

Attercliffe Vestry Hall

A typical evening was described in the *Independent* of 26 February, 1887:

The People's Entertainment Society. Another very successful entertainment was given on Saturday evening at the Attercliffe Vestry Hall by this society, the hall being crowded in every part, numbers seeking seats on the platform. The Master Cutler, (Mr. G.F. Lockwood), took the chair. The hit of the evening was undoubtably the solo playing of Mr. Hague on the concertina, his church bells, bagpipes and bird whistling being excellent.

Two other halls on Surrey Street – the Montgomery Hall and Mechanics' Institute

Of all the theatres and other places of entertainment, the Montgomery Hall proved to be one of the most durable and remains active to the present day in much the same form as when it first opened.

The Sheffield Sunday School Union launched the project in 1867, soon after the opening of the temperance hall in Townhead Street, for the use of the Union and similar organizations. The hall was a memorial to one of its most distinguished members, James Montgomery, newspaper editor, poet, and one of the most prolific of all nineteenth-century hymn writers. A site was secured in New Surrey Street and in July, 1884 the foundation stone was laid by A J Mundella, the MP for Brightside, one of the foremost politicians of his day. It was estimated that the cost would amount to some £15,000 − £5,000 for the site, about £8,000 for construction work and £2,000 for furnishings.

The Montgomery Hall — Still going strong today

The project had been carefully thought through. Shops were incorporated along the street frontage to provide rental income for the maintenance of the building. On the first floor the main hall could seat 1,000 people[*]. There was another decent sized hall with a capacity of 350, a large committee room for 120 people as well as numerous smaller committee rooms, class rooms, reading rooms, a ladies room and a library. Safety precautions were by far the best in Sheffield. All the corridors and staircases were fireproof, all the steps were full width and the doors opened outwards. Several

---

[*] The main hall is still in use as a theatre although its capacity is substantially reduced.

staircases led directly to the three entrances on Surrey Street so that in the event of fire the building could be evacuated quickly and easily.

It was made clear at the outset that all activities were to be in accordance with high moral standards. So there were plenty of performances of *Messiah* and other sacred music. Gradually, however, events of a lighter nature crept in. In 1889, Hartz, a well-known conjurer, appeared for two weeks followed by a diorama of the Paris Exhibition. From

1890 there were annual visits by the Victorian humorist George Grossmith, author of *The Diary of a Nobody* and a prominent member of the D'Oyly Carte Opera Company. His two-hour one-man show brought a glowing review from the *Independent* who praised his 'anecdote piled on anecdote each funnier than the last the like of which has rarely found expression within the Montgomery Hall'.[89] Prices rose to four shillings for George Grossmith and also for Jessie Bond and Rutland Barrington, two other stars from the D'Oyly Carte Opera.

George Grossmith provided some fun at the Montgomery

There was great excitement in 1891 when Edison's wonderful phonograph machine was demonstrated by C R C Steytler, of the Edison Phonograph Company. Stunned audiences listened to a reproduction of a speech by Gladstone, the sound of musical instruments plus some whistling and singing. A thrilling finale was provided by a recording of the band of the Coldstream Guards.

As the Victorian period began to draw to a close, a young lady turned up to take part in a 'grand Evening Concert' with a number of other students from the Royal College of Music. Her name was Clara Butt. We can only wonder if anyone in the audience realized that she would one day become one of the most famous contraltos of the early twentieth century.

Clara Butt

In 1847 a smart new building had opened on the corner of Tudor Street and Surrey Street. Inspired by Ebenezer Elliot, a group of enthusiasts had finally managed to raise enough money to build a Mechanics' Institute.

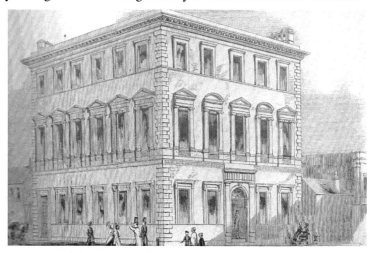

The Mechanics' Institute — a most impressive building

The aim, in common with similar institutions throughout the country, was to assist in the education of the working man. There were classrooms and study rooms, a library and a decent sized lecture hall which was big enough for concerts, balls and soirées. The building also housed a suite of rooms known as the 'Sheffield Athenaeum' a kind of gentleman's club[*].

Unfortunately the Mechanics' Institute and New Athenaeum was not destined for a long life. A new management took over and attempted to make money from what they now called the 'Lyceum Lecture Hall' but failed to make an impression. The Institute regained control in 1853, renamed it the 'Sheffield Mechanics' Institute Lecture Hall' and attempted to stick to its original plan to provide education for the working classes.[*] One of the first

---

[*] The choice of the name Athenaeum was unfortunate since just round corner in Norfolk Street there was another Athenaeum – a small, rather more exclusive club which organised concerts at the Music Hall in Surrey Street and other events at the Cutler's Hall. There were bound to be problems. In January 1851, the celebrated Fanny Kemble somehow managed to appear at the Music Hall under the auspices of the Norfolk Street Athenaeum, having originally been invited to Sheffield by the Athenaeum in Surrey Street!

events was 'Dramatic readings of Pure and Classical Authors'. Generally prices for this were on the high side with reserved seats ranging from sixpence to one shilling and sixpence. For 'Music for the People, oratorical music by Handel, Haydn and other masters', they were lower, even though these concerts were rather lavish affairs with over eighty performers.

The Institute's big moment came in 1855. Like Sheffield's Ebenezer Elliott, Charles Dickens knew what it was like to be at the bottom end of the social scale and he was an enthusiastic admirer of the work of the mechanics' institutes. On the 22 December, just in time for Christmas, he came to the Institute and gave his first public reading in Sheffield. It comes as no surprise to learn that the programme featured extracts from *A Christmas Carol*. Prices were high – five shillings for the best seats. The reading raised £80.7s. for the Institute's funds.[**]

This large donation must have helped it survive but the Institute continued to have serious financial problems. It struggled on for a while, managing to keep its 'People's Concerts' going – top price a shilling – always hoping to draw young people away from less salubrious venues around West Bar. But it never fully recovered from the crippling debts of the building's initial construction costs. In 1868, the Town Council took over the hall and turned it into a Council Chamber. The Institute still had access to the upper floor and occasional events were held there but its dreams of raising the cultural standards of Sheffield's underclass were over.

Other town-centre venues: the Assembly Rooms and the Cutlers' Hall

Back in 1762 when Sheffield decided that it needed a theatre it also felt the need to follow fashion and open assembly rooms as a place of recreation for

---

[*] The Lyceum, unable to advertise the hall as one of its amenities, suffered a terminal decline and was wound up in 1854. In May 1855, it gave up the former Lyceum accommodation. Redeveloped as Sheffield's first free public library, it opened on 1 February 1856. The site still forms part of the Sheffield Central Library building.

[**] Dickens later retained his fees for readings at the Music Hall. See page 100.

the increasing number of Sheffield's *nouveaux riches.* The Assembly Rooms and the Theatre were built on the same site and indeed for a number of years there seems to have been rather more enthusiasm for the Assembly Rooms than there was for the Theatre.[*] Social assemblies and dances for the well-to-do were held during the winter months and high prices ensured that they were very exclusive, very formal and very restrictive.

However, by the time Victoria came to the throne such rigid formality was no longer the fashion and the last assembly took place in the Rooms in 1846. After that they were used primarily for lectures, play readings, light entertainment and dancing. The playwright, J Sheridan Knowles gave four lectures there on the subject of 'Oratory and Dramatic Poetry' and F P Mude, one of Sheffield's favourite actors, stormed his way through six readings from Shakespeare. Seats for this one cost two shillings and one shilling. Then came evenings of Irish songs, stories and sketches including an appearance by the Royal Lilliputians a 'family of little people' who were very well received. But the Rooms had definitely lost their sparkle and in 1847 the Town Council took over the premises for use as a Council Room and Bankruptcy Court.

In 1868, the Council moved to the Mechanics Hall in Tudor Street and left the Rooms in a pretty poor state. The proprietors spruced it up, renamed it 'Assembly Rooms Building' and began a search for a new tenant. There were occasional dances and a handful of bookings. Chang, the Great Chinese Giant and his wife King Foo performed there and Dr Mason gave a talk in aid of the sick and wounded of the Franco-German war, including 'Reminiscences of a Fortnight in the German Hospitals'.

Chang and his family

The newly-formed St Peter's Club 'for tradesmen and clerks' took over the tenancy in 1872 but failed financially. In 1883,[**] the Arundel Club moved in but it too ran out of funds. The building was repossessed in 1885

---

[*] The Assembly Rooms faced onto Norfolk Street.
[**] The Club appears to have used the premises before that. They put on a 'dramatic entertainment' there in 1881.

and, after more than a hundred and twenty years, the Assembly Rooms' days as a place of entertainment were finally over.

The Cutlers' Hall

There was rather more going on at the headquarters of the Company of Cutlers of Hallamshire.[*] The Cutlers' Hall in Church Street was built in 1832 and soon became an opulent venue for a fashionable evening out. A large banqueting room, added in 1867, served as a concert hall and by the 1870s it was attracting good audiences. It was large enough to accommodate the Royal Italian Opera Company who appeared under the auspices of the Athenaeum Club. The Hall also catered for the flourishing Christmas concert market and on Christmas Day 1893,

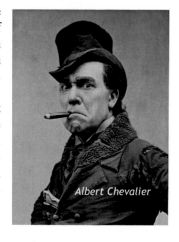

Albert Chevalier

---

[*] There were previous halls on the same site, built in 1638 and 1725. The present building was designed by Samuel Worth and Benjamin Broomhead Taylor, with later extensions by Flockton and Abbot and J B Mitchell Withers.

156

it offered sacred music by Mlle Hirsch's Anglo-Viennese Ladies Orchestra.

Surprisingly, this august building also occasionally hosted visits from music hall acts such as 'the wonderful people, the Botocudos Indians', Marian 'the Giant Amazon Queen accompanied by Colonel Olpts the midget', and 'Harvey's Little Folks'. And indeed there were one or two big names. Music hall star Albert Chevalier drew large audiences for his famous cockney character impersonations and songs, in particular, the tear-jerking 'My old Dutch.' These attractions were not quite what you would expect to find at the Cutlers' Hall – but they were extremely popular.

*As Victoria's long reign drew to a
close there were signs that things
were changing*

Finale

*Entertainment in Sheffield gets ready
for the twentieth century*

The City Theatre opens

In 1893, the ageing Alexandra and the aged Theatre Royal found themselves facing competion from a smart, new, up-to-date theatre. Since 1892, Alexander Stacey had been staging popular sensation plays and melodramas at his Grand Circus in Tudor Street. For many years the building had functioned as a rather large music hall but clearly Stacey now had other ideas. Tudor Street, right in the centre of town, would be an ideal place to build a theatre but first he had to clear the site. In the spring of 1893, fate gave him a helping hand. The Circus staged *On the Frontier,* a play which featured a spectacular fire. And on 30 May, at three thirty in the morning, the wooden building burnt down. Overall Stacey lost around £500 – a substantial amount but by no means crippling. He moved quickly. The charred remains were removed and at the end of July a foundation stone was laid by Augustus Harris. Building then began at break-neck speed and, on Boxing Day 1893, the 'City Theatre', named in honour of Sheffield's new status, opened its doors. There had been no time to rehearse a money-making pantomime so the City's first production was a touring show, *A Royal Divorce* by W G Wills and Grace Hawthorn.

The City Theatre, which became the Lyceum, was right next to the Royal

Not surprisingly the opening of a brand new theatre caused quite a stir. Although both the Royal and the Alexandra had undergone a number of structural changes there was no getting away from the fact that one was now a hundred and thirty years old and the other had just had its sixty fifth birthday. The City Theatre, lit by electricity, was full of the most up to date equipment. To a public fearful of theatre fires it must have been reassuring to read that the building was 'perfectly fireproof' and that 'safety was guaranteed by numerous exits, 10 monster hydrants, thousands of water sprinklers, and a new arrangement of asbestos curtains.'[90] The new theatre had its own box office where private boxes could be booked at two pounds two shillings, dress circle seats three shillings, the side circle two shillings, and pit stalls one shilling. The pit at sixpence and the gallery at fourpence were unreserved.

Even though *A Royal Divorce* had been seen before in Sheffield and also had to compete with the annual pantomimes at the Royal and the Alexandra, its short run of five evening performances and two matinees was quickly sold out. The *Independent* reported that all the streets around the new theatre were blocked and it was estimated that the gallery, built for a 1,000 people, held 1,140 on the opening night.

And what of the play itself? The *Independent* was enthusiastic. Henry Vibart's representation of Napoleon was

a study in itself, a finer bit of character sketching having been seldom seen on the stage. Miss Bertie Willis (as Josephine) made a charming and loveable heroine, who, gaining the sympathies of the audience at an early stage in the performance, held them in close touch till the closing scenes. Mr H. G. Dolby scored heavily in the part of Talleyrand, and the other members of the company..... met with the most enthusiastic reception. The architectural beauties and the acoustic properties of the theatre were universally admired, and Mr Stacey was heartily complimented on his handsome addition to Sheffield's playhouses.[91]

The 'City' had got off to an excellent start.

There is little doubt that the opening of this new playhouse was highly significant. Now, for the first time Sheffield had three 'legitimate' theatres all in direct competition with one another. A new era had begun. Sheffield was ready for the twentieth century.

Postscript - the final years of Victoria's reign

A vibrant, bustling city with an expanding popuation was now an attractive proposition. In 1895, the Empire, a gigantic music hall which could seat over 3,000 people, opened on Charles Street. It provided real competition for Sheffield's mainstream theatres and killed off a good many smaller music halls.

However, equally significant was the subsequent development of the City Theatre. In 1896, the Sheffield Lyceum Theatre Company Limited, a specially formed consortium, persuaded Alexander Stacey to part with his brand new playhouse. This new group certainly meant business – it had a capital of £25,000 in £10 shares and was obviously in a position to make Stacey an offer he could not refuse. The theatre reopened under the new management in January, 1897 – then closed again at Easter for extensive alterations and reconstruction. Although quite a lot of the fabric of the original City building remained, the transformation was spectacular. The Company had commissioned an outstanding young theatre architect, W G R Sprague, and suddenly Sheffield had one of the most exciting theatres in the country. The elaborate auditorium, restored to its former glory in 1990, gives today's theatregoers some idea of the thrill that first audience must have felt when, on Monday 11 October 1897, they entered the Lyceum for the first time and sat among the cherubs watching the Carl Rosa company perform Bizet's *Carmen*.

There was a final change to the theatrical scene when the Lyceum company took over the running of the Royal. As Victoria's reign finally came to an end Sheffield had three major theatres, two of which, side by side in a prime location, were working together under one management. It all looked very promising.

Notes

1 *Sheffield and Rotherham Independent (hereafter cited as 'Independent')* 10.10.1846
2 *Independent* 29.10.1853
3 *Independent* 13.11.1858
4 *Independent* 1.6. 1861
5 *Independent* 21.4.1864
6 *Independent* 11.3.1863
7 *Independent* 30.7.1864
8 *Independent* 28.10.1870
9 *Independent* 15.8.1871
10 *Independent* 22.6.1872
11 *Independent* 25.8.1874
12 *Independent* 25.8.1874
13 *Independent* 17.4.1875
14 *Independent* 13.7.1876
15 *Independent* 2.11.1880
16 *Independent* 2.11.1880
17 *Independent* 27.6.1882
18 *Independent* 13.10.1885
19 *Independent* 31.6.1886
20 *Independent* 5.8.1893
21 *Independent* 29.8.1893
22 *Independent* 24.12.1847
23 *Independent* 8.7.1848
24 *Independent* 16.12.1848
25 *Independent* 24.2.1849
26 *Independent* 30.9.1854
27 *Independent* 10.9.1858
28 *Independent* 1.5.1858
29 *Independent* 13.10.1865
30 *Independent* 14. 10.1865
31 *Independent* 21.7.1874
32 *Independent* 15.1.1876
33 *Independent* 22.4.1879
34 *Independent* 22.11.1879 and 29.9.1879
35 *Independent* 6.7.1880
36 *Independent* 11.7.1882
37 *Independent* 18.3.1888
38 *Independent* 27.9.1893
39 *Independent* 6.5.1890
40 *Independent* 29.8.1893
41 *Independent* 29.8.1893
42 *Independent* 29.11.1845
43 *Independent* 20.10.1849
44 *Independent* 18.11.1893
45 *Independent* 30.5.1893
46 *Independent* 24 .2.1865

48 *Independent* 19.10.1886
49 *Independent* 10.3.1849
50 *Independent* 5.4.1856
51 *Independent* 28.3.1862
52 *Independent* 24.10.1861
53 *Independent* 13 .12. 1862
54 *Independent* 16.3.1869
55 *Independent* 7.12.1875
56 *Independent* 4.9.1852
57 *Independent* 26.2.1859
58 *Independent* 26.3.1859
59 *Independent* 6.12.1845
60 *Independent* 2.1.1877
61 *Independent* 17.11.1866
62 *Independent* 10.4.1866
63 *Independent* 28.12.1875
64 *Independent* 16.11.1867
65 *Independent* 2 .5.1876
66 *Independent* 3.9.1870
67 *Independent* 13.12.1873
68 *Independent* 16.2.1874
69 *Independent* 29.9.1874
70 *Independent* 13.10.1874
71 *Independent* 18.1.1875
72 *Independent* 18.1.1875
73 *Independent* 29.12.1875
74 *Sheffield Daily Telegraph* 12 .1. 1877
75 *Independent* 17.4.1877
76 *Independent* 22.11.1878
77 *Independent* 3.5.1887
78 *Independent* 7.11.1889
79 *Independent* 19.12.1893
80 *Independent* 23.10.1872
81 *Independent* 26.12.1888
82 *Independent* 20.11.1874
83 *Independent* 1.5.1877
84 *Independent* 27.3.1883
85 *Independent* 11.8.1891
86 *Sheffield History Reporter,* Issue 67, December 1999 / January 2000
87 *Independent* 26.12.1885
88 *Independent* 22.10.1890
89 *Independent* 8.3.1890
90 *Independent* 19.12.1893
91 *Independent* 27.12.1893

Appendix

The Theatres Acts

In 1737 the Prime Minister, Horace Walpole, heavily criticised by satirists like John Gay and Henry Fielding, attempted to ensure that the stage should not be used for political protest. This led to a new Act of Parliament.

The Licensing Act 1737

From now on spoken drama could only be performed at one of the two 'Patent' London playhouses, the Theatre Royal Covent Garden and the Theatre Royal Drury Lane. The Act's main aim was to control theatre in London.   Later licences were granted to a number of larger provisional companies.

It was standard practice to include music in all productions thus ensuring that they were not 'spoken drama'.

The Act gave the Lord Chamberlain the power to vet all new plays and refuse to allow them to be performed if he considered that they were unsuitable.   He also had the power to close down a play if he was unhappy with the way it was being performed. This form of censorship was not removed until 1968 by which time the Lord Chamberlain was not so much looking for attacks on the government of the day but aimed to make sure that naughty words or, worse still, naughty scenes did not upset the more puritanical members of the audience.

The Theatrical Representations Act of 1788

This gave magistrates the authority to license occasional performances for up to sixty days.

The Theatres Act 1843

This did away with many of the 1737 restrictions – but until 1968 performances of all plays still required the Lord Chamberlain's approval.

Select Bibliography

Archer, William, *The Old Drama and the New*, London 1923

Barker, Kathleen M D, *Dance and the Emerging Music Hall in the Provinces*

Bland, Fred, Ed., *Collection of Documents relating to Local History of Sheffield*, Sheffield City Archives Ref BC 15-1

Booth , Michael , *Hiss the Villain*, London,1964

Brooks, Peter, *The Melodramatic Imagination* , Newhaven 1976

Dickens, Charles, *Hard Times,* reprinted Penguin Books, London 1994

Hartnoll, Phylis ed ., *Oxford Companion to the Theatre*, Oxford 1962

Irving, Laurence, *Henry Irving The Actor and His World*, London 1951

Leno, Dan , *Dan Leno: hys booke : a volume of frivolities: autobiographical, historical ...* London, 1901

Hillerby, Bryen D, *Lost Theatres of Sheffield* , Warncliffe Publishing, Sheffield, 1999

Lewis, Samuel, *A Topographical Dictionary of England,* 1835

Rowell, George ed., Nineteenth Century Plays , Oxford   1972

Sheffield History Research Group, *Georgian Theatre in Sheffield,* Sheffield   2003

Shepherd, Richard Herne, *The Plays and Poems of Charles Dickens*, London 1885

Sheffield and Rotherham Red Book, 1883

Sheffield Theatre and Assembly Rooms Minute Book, Sheffield City Archives, Ref CA 373 1-4

Styan , J L, *The English Stage* , Cambridge 1996

The Builder, 5 October 1861 and 9 October 1897

The Illustrated Guide to Sheffield, 1879

Trewin, J C, *Mr Macready. A Nineteenth-century Tragedian and his Theatre,* London 1955

Vandenhoff, George, *An Actor's Notebook or the Green Room,* London 1865

Vickers, J Edward, *A Popular History of Sheffield*, Sheffield 1992

Ward ,Geneviève and Whiteing, Richard, *Both Sides of the Curtain* , London 1918

Performers and Personalities

vii

Theatres, halls and other venues

Plays, Operas and Oratorios

Circuses, Choirs, Bands, Orchestras, animals and other acts

XV

General Index